T0113830

Land Without Thunder and other stories

AFRICAN CLASSICS SERIES

1. *Secret Lives* – Ngugi wa Thiong'o
2. *Matigari* – Ngugi wa Thiong'o
3. *A Grain of Wheat* – Ngugi wa Thiong'o
4. *Weep Not, Child* – Ngugi wa Thiong'o
5. *The River Between* – Ngugi wa Thiong'o
6. *Devil on the Cross* – Ngugi wa Thiong'o
7. *Petals of Blood* – Ngugi wa Thiong'o
8. *Wizard of the Crow* – Ngugi wa Thiong'o
9. *Homing In* – Marjorie Oludhe Macgoye
10. *Coming to Birth* – Marjorie Oludhe Macgoye
11. *Street Life* – Marjorie Oludhe Macgoye
12. *The Present Moment* – Marjorie Oludhe Macgoye
13. *Chira* – Marjorie Oludhe Macgoye
14. *A Farm Called Kishinev* – Marjorie Oludhe Macgoye
15. *No Longer at Ease* – Chinua Achebe
16. *Arrow of God* – Chinua Achebe
17. *A Man of the People* – Chinua Achebe
18. *Things Fall Apart* – Chinua Achebe
19. *Anthills of the Savannah* – Chinua Achebe
20. *The Strange Bride* – Grace Ogot
21. *Land Without Thunder* – Grace Ogot
22. *The Promised Land* – Grace Ogot
23. *The Other Woman* – Grace Ogot
24. *The Minister's Daughter* – Mwangi Ruheni
25. *The Future Leaders* – Mwangi Ruheni
26. *White Teeth* – Okot P'Bitek
27. *Horn of My Love* – Okot P'Bitek
28. *God's Bits of Wood* – Sembene Ousmane
29. *Emperor Shaka the Great* – Masizi Kunene
30. *No Easy Walk to Freedom* – Nelson Mandela
31. *Mine Boy* – Peter Abrahams
32. *Takadini* – Ben Hanson
33. *Myths and Legends of the Swahili* – Jan Knappert
34. *Mau Mau Author in Detention* – Gakaara wa Wanjau
35. *Igereka and Other African Narratives* – John Ruganda
36. *Kill Me Quick* – Meja Mwangi
37. *Going Down River Road* – Meja Mwangi
38. *Striving for the Wind* – Meja Mwangi
39. *Carcase for Hounds* – Meja Mwangi
40. *The Last Plague* – Meja Mwangi
41. *The Big Chiefs* – Meja Mwangi
42. *The Slave* – Elechi Amadi
43. *The Concubine* – Elechi Amadi
44. *The Great Ponds* – Elechi Amadi
45. *The African Child* – Camara Laye

PEAK LIBRARY SERIES

1. *Without a Conscience* – Barbara Baumann
2. *The Herdsman's Daughter* – Bernard Chahilu
3. *Hearthstones* – Kekelwa Nyaywa
4. *Of Man and Lion* – Beatrice Erlwanger
5. *My Heart on Trial* – Genga Idowu
6. *Kosiya Kifefe* – Arthur Gakwandi
7. *Return to Paradise* – Yusuf K Dawood
8. *Mission to Gehenna* – Karanja wa Kang'ethe
9. *Goatsmell* – Nevanji Madanhire
10. *Sunset in Africa* – Peter M Nyarango
11. *The Moon Also Sets* – Osi Ogbu
12. *Breaking Chains* – Dorothea Holi
13. *The Missing Links* – Tobias O Otieno
14. *I Shall Walk Alone* – Paul Nakitare
15. *A Season of Waiting* – David Omowale
16. *Before the Rooster Crows* – Peter Kimani
17. *A Nose for Money* – Francis B Nyamnjoh
18. *The Travail of Dieudonné* – Francis B Nyamnjoh
19. *A Journey Within* – Florence Mbaya
20. *The Doomed Conspiracy* – Barrack O Muluka and Tobias O Otieno
21. *The Lone Dancer* – Joe Kiarie
22. *Eye of the Storm* – Yusuf K Dawood
23. *Animal Farm* – George Orwell
24. *Stillborn* – Diekoye Oyeyinka
25. *Ugandan Affairs* – Sira Kiwana
26. *African Quilt* – Harshi Syal Gill and Parvin D. Syal
27. *The Dolphin Catchers and other stories*
28. *Black Ghost* – Ken N. Kamoche
29. *The Guardian Angels* – Issa Noor

Land Without Thunder
and Other Stories

Grace Ogot

East African
Educational Publishers Ltd.
Nairobi • Kampala • Dar es Salaam • Kigali • Lilongwe • Lusaka

Published by
East African Educational Publishers Ltd.
Kijabe Street, Nairobi
P.O. Box 45314, Nairobi – 00100, KENYA
Tel: +254 20 2324760
Mobile: +254 722 205661 / 722 207216 / 733 677716 / 734 652012
Email: eaep@eastafricanpublishers.com
Website: www.eastafricanpublishers.com

East African Educational Publishers also has offices or is represented in the following
countries: Uganda, Tanzania, Rwanda, Malawi, Zambia, Botswana and South Sudan.

First published in 1968 by
East African Publishing House

First Published by
East African Educational Publishers in 1988

Reprinted six times
(reformatted), 2004, 2008

This impression 2014
Reprinted 2017

ISBN 978-9966-46-588-X

Printed in Kenya by
Autolitho Limited

Contents

The Old White Witch...1

The Bamboo Hut 16

The Hero...25

Tekayo...31

Karantina 42

The Green Leaves 63

The Empty Basket 72

The white veil..79

Land Without Thunder 102

The Rain Came...116

Night Sister 126

Elizabeth...137

The Old White Witch

The chapel was fuller than usual that morning. Matron Jack and Sister Cocks sat with their heads lowered in silent prayer. But the nurses, as if unaware of the holiness of the house of God, wore defiant faces as they waited impatiently for the service to start. When Norman Eland, the hospital superintendent, entered the chapel to take his place among the senior members of staff, the sullen nurses cleared their throats while others jeered at him. But Norman ignored the accusing looks that followed him and walked majestically to his seat.

The big clock struck ten and Matron Jack rose to announce the hymn. As her voice died out, the staff got up to sing, led by Sister Cocks at the organ.

> *When I survey the wondrous cross*
> *On which the Prince of Glory died*
> *My richest gain I count but loss ...*

Matron Jack went scarlet with fury. The nurses were not singing, and hymn-books remained unopened on the benches before them. Only the masculine voices of the male nurses and senior staff, together with that of the Rev Odhuno, filled the chapel and drowned the sound of the old organ. Behind them, cooks and cleaners stood with blank faces staring at the books they could not read. Why were these women so stubborn and defiant? As Matron asked herself this question she wished God could sometimes punish the disobedient in the manner He dealt with the godless inhabitants of Sodom and Gomorrah or the covetous wife of Lot. When the hymn ended, the nurses sat down noisily. They dragged wooden benches on the cement floor, so that when Dr Joseph got up to read St Matthew Chapter 12, his nerves were already on edge, and his anger was only matched by that of Matron Jack who sat opposite the heathen and ungrateful native nurses whose hearts, she was sure, were filled with the venom of poisonous snakes. Dr Joseph read the lesson clearly. Most of the nurses refused to open their Bibles, yet it was for their benefit that he had chosen that particular text. He read:

A sower went out to sow. And as he sowed, some seed fell along the footpath; and the birds came and ate it up. Some fell on rocky ground, where it had little soil, it sprouted quickly because it had no depth of earth, but when the sun rose the young corn was scorched, and as it had no root it withered away. Some seed fell among thistles; and the thistles shot up, and choked the corn. And some of the seed fell into good soil, where it bore fruit, yielding a hundredfold, or it might be sixtyfold or thirtyfold. If you have ears, then hear.

The morning service ended, and was followed by a special meeting of the hospital senior staff. The Matron spoke first. She was troubled in her mind and her hands quivered with every movement of her lips. Mr Jairo Okumu who was in charge of the outpatients' department translated for her. She told the nurses that they were stupid to organise a strike meeting because they had been asked to give their own people a bedpan. She and Sister Cocks had trained in a great hospital in England, a hospital with a long tradition and an international reputation. From the day she started her training, she was made to understand that giving a bedpan to a patient was part of a nurse's job, and it was as important as feeding or bathing a patient. Matron Jack went on to say how horrified she was to find on her arrival at Magwar Hospital that men sweepers gave bedpans to woman patients, while the nurses stood idly looking on. This was a barbaric practice and it could not be tolerated in a mission hospital. She had therefore decided to stop it.

"I am not the only one who feels strongly about this. Senior members of staff are behind me. From now onwards every nurse in this hospital must carry a bedpan. We must learn to serve our fellow women whom we can see in order to love and serve God whom we cannot see."

Loud whispers broke from the nurses benches, drowning the Matron's voice. Some were jeering, while others were muttering, "Judas Iscariots, traitors," to the server male members of the staff who had been exposed as supporters of the new regulation by the Matron.

"There is no need for jeering," Matron told the girls angrily. "We will not stay with you forever, spoon-feeding you like children. Having accepted Christ, you must face the challenge and lead your people who are still walking in darkness and are governed by taboos and superstitions." She hesitated a while, and then demanded, "Where is Monica, the head girl? I can't have my nurses behaving like this in the house of God – I am ashamed of you." But when Monica Adhiambo got up, she ignored the Matron's warnings.

"Long before you came, we agreed to nurse in this hospital on the understanding that we were not to carry bedpans. We want to be married and become mothers like any other women in the land. We are surprised that senior members of the staff have sneaked behind us to support you, when they know perfectly well that no sane man will agree to marry a woman who carries a bedpan. A special class of people do this job in our society. Your terms are therefore unacceptable, Matron. You can keep your hospital and the sick. And if being a Christian means carrying faeces and urine, you can keep Christianity too – we are returning to our homes."

Dr Joseph looked at Nurse Adhiambo unbelievingly. He was astonished that these simple, semi-educated native girl could be so darling and outspoken. Had the proverbial seven devils entered into Adhiambo's head?

The awkward silence persisted, and Matron Jack was stunned. She looked at the senior male African staff appealingly. Then all eyes were turned to Rev Odhuno, who was often called Solomon because of his wise counsel. Rev Odhuno moved fearlessly from the back towards the altar. He looked upon these girls as his children – he was old enough to be their father, and he was also the head of their church. The girls were therefore likely to treat him with deference. His presence at the altar eased the tension a little.

Rev Odhuno was a man of God. The nurses liked him because he was fatherly and pure in heart. To the European members of staff, he was Solomon incarnate – arbitrator and judge in difficult cases. But many people doubted the sincerity of the Europeans in their professed faith in the impartiality and wisdom of Rev Odhuno. It was said, for instance, that each time the Pastor was asked for a cup of tea at Dr Joseph's house, Mrs Joseph boiled the cup afterwards, or soaked it in Jeyes for twenty-four hours. These and many other stories reached Rev Odhuno's ears, but he dismissed them tightly. He told his colleagues that a man of God should not listen to the wagging tongue of the devil who was roaming the land looking for weak minds in which to plant the seeds of hatred and destruction.

"My children, how can you behave like this in the house of God? You may have genuine grievances. You may disagree with the hospital authorities and refuse to do what they tell you, but you are Christians. On your baptism day you proclaimed publicly that you will renounce the devil and all his works, and that you will eschew the vain pomp and glory of the world." He paused to let his words sink down.

"Listen to me carefully, my children," he continued. "You are all grown-up women. The country put you here so that you may heal the sick and comfort the dying. God has blessed you, and has called you to witness for Him by carrying on the noble work He himself started while He was on earth. Is it not written that he who puts hands on the plough should not look back? Are you prepared to turn your backs on the Almighty Lord? Let not the devil mislead you – stay on and serve your master. For Christ said, 'Whatsoever you do to one of these little ones, you do it unto the Lord.' Obey God's call – return to your rooms change into your uniforms and continue to work in the Lord's vineyard."

Nurse Adhiambo was clutching a note that had been passed to her from behind. She glanced at it and folded it again. It had no signature, and because it was written in capital letters, she could not detect whose handwriting it was. The note said:

> *TELL HIM THAT ON THE DAY OF OUR BAPTISM WHEN WE PROCLAIMED PUBLICLY THAT WE WILL RENOUNCE THE DEVIL WITH ALL HIS WORKS, WE DID NOT PROCLAIM THAT WE WILL CARRY URINE AND FAECES OF FELLOW HUMAN BEINGS. TELL HIM WE ARE GETTING LATE.*

Nurse Adhiambo looked at the note again and then at the Matron and Rev Odhuno who had come to the end of his speech, but courage deserted her. She tried to get up to tell Rev Odhuno the contents of the note, but something glued her to her seat. Like the others she timidly watched the pastor return to her place.

Then Dr Joseph announced that, because of the additional responsibility that was being placed upon the nurses, they would have their pay increased from 6/- to 7.50/= a month. This, he was sure, would go a long way towards helping the young women to meet the numerous demands from their families and relatives. And he invited Nurse Adhiambo and two more of her colleagues to meet the Senior Administrative Staff to formalise the agreement.

The nurses wriggled out of the chapel door in great haste as though some unknown forces; were driving them out. Then a tremendous laughter broke out among them as soon as they got clear of the chapel ground. They shouted and jeered as they rushed towards their dormitory.

They had passed the wards now, and they turned in at the gate that led into the 'holy of holies'. This was the name that had been given to the barricaded Nurses' Home by the young men who were never allowed in. The door of the dormitory stood open, and they entered the main hall of this big building which in the past housed both general and maternity patients.

"Listen to me all of you!" Nurse Adhiambo stood on the chair. "Our last night's plans are final. Let a curse be upon whoever betrays us at such a late hour and joins hands with the Administrators."

"Yeah," the nurses answered in a chorus of wild laughter.

"If we stick together," Nurse Adhiambo continued, "these do-gooders like Jack and Cocks will soon succumb to our wishes. Is it not true that they give orders while we work? Then let them carry urine and faeces – they will not do it for a week. When they are desperate, and the work is too heavy for them, they will call us back, on our own terms. Now let us say goodbye to one another, take our luggage and move out in a group. The God of Rev Odhuno will go with you."

"Amen!" the girls shouted.

Then the exodus began.

Nurse Adhiambo took her box and a basket containing a few items and stood in the doorway, while the other nurses streamed out of the hall. When Adhiambo was satisfied that no one had changed her mind or taken hospital property, she put her wooden box on her head and followed her colleagues.

The nurses took the narrow footpath that passed between the laundry and the women's wards. It then ran parallel to the men's wards and the theatre. The chapel stood some distance away from them all – deliberately to allow the staff to worship in peace. The nurses were not shouting any more, but the pata-pata of their footsteps attracted the attention of patients and workmen, and they came out in full force. Some workmen shouted their disapproval, while others cheered. But most of the patients only wept.

"Shame to see them leaving us sick and helpless," said a woman's voice.

"That doctor is good," another patient put in. "It is that granny who is spoiling things; since she came to this hospital, everything has been standing on its head. The old Mrs Ainsworth knew our customs – she was kind to the girls and did not discourage them from getting married. But this one wants all our young girls to remain *bikra* like herself."

The Head Cook ran to the chapel to look for the Matron. He flung the chapel door open and bubbled out the first thing that came to his mind.

"*Yote nakwenda*, Matron, *yote.*" "What *nakwenda*, Nimrod?" The Matron sounded angry. She was in the middle of negotiating a very delicate point with the senior members of staff before summoning the nurses' representatives, and here was Nimrod with his small brain interrupting the proceedings merely to tell her that all the women who bring vegetables to sell had gone away. "*Kwenda* kitchen, Nimrod, no more *shauri sasa,*" and she waved the Head Cook off with her hand. Then she turned round to face Dr Joseph, who had been making a point when Nimrod intervened.

A pang of bitterness flared up in Nimrod's heart – nurses were not his responsibility. But he knew that if the nurses left, he and his staff would have to distribute food to some fifty ailing persons and to feed the helpless ones. He was not prepared to work himself to death, much as he dreaded unemployment. Out of his own kindness he had come to inform this bikra that her girls were going away – and she was just quarrelling. "Matron, *shauri yako,*" Nimrod threw his hands in the air. "Nurse *yote yote nakwenda, nakwisha chukua sanduku.*" Nimrod banged the door and left.

"Did you hear that?" Matron Jack turned to Dr Joseph and the staff. She was already on her feet, heading for the door. "Did you hear that, Arnold? All the nurses are going with their luggage."

The Matron rushed out of the chapel, followed by Dr Arnold Joseph and the senior members of staff together with Rev Odhuno.

The whole hospital was in commotion. Patients were out of the wards, and workmen were dotted all over the compound with pangas in their hands. At first it looked like a huge joke until the Matron's eyes rested on a procession of women along the Hospital Road carrying wooden boxes on their heads. It resembled a funeral procession.

"Run after them! Catch them!" Matron Jack shouted at the top of her voice to the idle workmen.

Dr Joseph looked indifferent and his attitude irritated Matron Jack who now looked anxious. A group of workers were running after the nurses and were almost overtaking them. She wanted to run too, but old age was catching up with her, and the high heeled shoes she wore that morning limited her pace. The rest of the senior members of staff together with Rev Odhuno were walking close behind her, talking among themselves.

"This is a terrible thing Rev Odhuno," Issaca rebuked the Father. "You and I know that this new rule which enjoins that our girls should carry karaya is wrong. You should not have sided with these administrators publicly – that was bad."

"Wait a minute, Issaca. I cautioned Matron Jack and Dr Joseph that even Christian women will not agree to carry *karaya* – but they insisted now when the matter is out of hand they want my assistance. You can see my dilemma, my brother – I couldn't get up publicly in the house of God and side with these nurses. We should give our missionaries support – they are so few! I know you understand."

"We feel hurt all the same, Father. The nurses are calling us traitors. You remember the scene in the chapel earlier today."

"Yeah." He felt hot and uncomfortable under the holy collar.

The girls had been halted by workers who stood before them, with pangas. They were cursing and using abusive words. The appearance of Rev Odhuno quietened them for a while.

"You are wasting our time," Nurse Adhiambo said, stepping forward, "You send men with pangas after us, as if we are thieves!"

She refused to address the Matron this time, instead she directed her words to the senior staff who accompanied the Matron.

"We will not carry *karaya* now or in future. Tell Matron Jack and her people that we are returning home to help our mothers in the shambas and to get married."

"Don't talk like that," shouted Matron Jack. She was bubbling over with rage. She stepped forward and grabbed Nurse Adhiambo's hand, dragging her out of the group. The girl staggered and almost dropped her wooden box, but somehow she managed to retain her balance. She put her feet together and disengaged herself from the old woman's weak grip.

"You are the cause of all these *fitina*," Matron Jack waved a fist at her. "The hospital selected you to be the head girl because you are a keen Christian, educated and a good worker. Now all we get back is a slap on the face. You organised a strike against us."

"Keep your head girl, I have left it in the dormitory," Nurse Adhiambo replied rudely. "Give it to someone here."

The Matron continued to talk as if she did not hear Nurse Adhiambo's words. "All right my child," she lowered her voice. "It is no good quarrelling like this. I want each one of you to return to the dormitory to hand in hospital property – each one of you, understand." She stood waiting.

"Adhiambo and Wamakobe will go with you," one of the older girls now spoke.

"We left everything behind – everything from uniforms to dustbin."

"No, I want all of you to come back to the dormitory," Matron Jack commanded.

But the girls shouted back. "None of us will come except Adhiambo and Wamakobe. We do not want to trot up and down with boxes."

The morning had started badly, Matron Jack felt it was beneath her dignity to argue with people she regarded as primitive, ignorant and irreligious. Even senior men like Issaca, Norman and Jairo, who were supposed to safeguard the interests of the hospital, simply stood there and did nothing! Would the missionaries ever succeed in winning Africa for Christ?

After some persuasion from Rev Odhuno, Adhiambo and Wamakobe agreed to turn to the dormitory to hand things over officially to the Matron. "Return to your work, you lazy creatures," Matron shouted to the workmen. The men obeyed her instantly. Judging by the looks on their faces, it was evident that they had enjoyed every minute of the spectacle.

They were now cutting grass between the theatre and the kitchen. Matron Jack avoided their direction. She wished the African women folk were as obedient as their men. She had been told again and again that African men were little Caesars who treated their women like slaves. But why was it that she found the men cooperative and obedient? It was these headstrong females whom she found impossible to work with.

The door of the nurses' hall stood open and they entered. The long dining table was covered with neatly arranged clothing. That at least impressed Matron beyond words. But she could not say so now, the rebellious girls did not deserve any thanks from her. She looked at the clothing from row to row – everything was there. Then she checked all the items – they were all there. She examined everything and every nook assiduously with the hope of finding a pretext for delaying the nurses' departure. But none could be found.

Adhiambo and Wamakobe left. They did not say goodbye to the Matron whom they left standing alone in the doorway. They walked on without looking back, waving triumphantly to the workmen, who wished them good luck. They found the rest of the nurses waiting for them at the end of the Hospital Road. In a boisterous and jubilant manner, they yelled byebye to one another. They now felt free from the iron rule of the old spinster.

Matron Jack locked the door slowly and walked back to her bungalow which she shared with Sister Cocks. She knew she was needed at the hospital to sort out the chaos. Beds were not made, medicines were not given, several maternity patients were perhaps in agony ready to give birth, and the wet babies were wailing everywhere. The noise disturbed her. She needed a peaceful atmosphere for quiet meditation, and she knew this was only obtainable in her cosy room whose curtains and bedspread she had brought from England. The room was cool and peaceful. On the wooden cupboard near the bedside, the Bible, the Hymn Book and the Daily Light all stared at her. She fixed her eyes on them for a moment, then a faint smile radiated off the corner of her mouth, the kind of dry smile a desperate person gives even in a forlorn situation. The words that she had read in the Daily Light that morning came to her mind. *Call upon me at the time of need and I will deliver thee.*

The words had sounded so true when she read them. She had loved God and believed in those words ever since she was a baby. For the past week she had wept and called upon the Lord many times to make the native nurses abandon the idea of a strike. Does God answer our prayers? The people to whom they had brought Christianity had now won; and those who had walked in the fight all their lives had been deserted by God in the hour of need!

A tap at the door startled her. She turned round. "What is it, Teresa?" She did not sound angry, she was just dejected.

"Lunch *tayari* Matron, *Dr Joseph na Mama Joseph nakwisha fika.*"

"Christ," she put her hand on her chest, "of all the days, the Josephs would come to lunch today." Why did she call them? Mrs Joseph with her wagging tongue would talk of nothing but the strike, the natives, the houseboys, the shamba boy and what have you – she never seemed to get tired of complaining about the natives. Matron Jack sighed and went to the mirror to tidy her hair. She had no appetite, and she felt sick.

An emergency meeting was held in the afternoon to review the steadily deteriorating situation. There was a great danger of epidemics. Bits of food were scattered everywhere in the unswept wards – some children had urinated and defecated on the floor, while the helpless patients lay in wet bed clothes. During lunch time, Dr Joseph had taken Matron aside and told her flatly that she was responsible for the chaos.

"If you do not modify your ideas, you will have to go back to England," he warned her. "It will be a good thousand years before you can apply your English training to these native hospitals. When you are talking about nurses carrying bedpans, you think of some well-educated English women with four years nursing training. You forget the simple fact that these young girls only wear a thin veneer of civilisation. Scratch them deep enough and you find a real savage."

He walked away leaving Matron Jack helpless and brokenhearted.

Most members of staff were there now Jairo, Norman, Issaca and Dr Joseph. Only Rev Odhuno was not there and Sister Cocks was still held up in the maternity ward. The atmosphere was tense and Matron Jack sat on the edge of a chair waiting patiently for Dr Joseph to speak.

The discussion lasted about forty minutes, after which it was resolved that there must not be any more admissions into the women's wards and the maternity, and that all able bodied women patients in both wards should be discharged that very afternoon and that the very sick ones should be discharged within the next two to three days.

Meanwhile, two male nurses were to be seconded to help in the general women's wards and Sister Cocks would look after the maternity ward till all the waiting mothers were delivered. The kitchen staff would distribute the food as best they could and Okebe and Okwamba, who were already sacked, would carry on with the work of giving bedpans as they did before.

The African members of staff did not say much. In a way they were happy that the women had gone on strike. Matron Jack had been treating them like little children. They were never consulted on anything, and she was always supported, at least publicly, by her fellow Europeans.

The women and maternity wards were closed. Sister Cocks helped in the outpatient's department where the number of attendants had doubled after the nurses strike.

Several European missionaries from the headquarters visited the hospital. They all advised against the bedpan regulation. It was difficult enough to recruit new nurses, and to insist on the new regulation would mean that the profession would eaxy a social stigma in the eyes of the Africans from which it might not recover for a long time.

The dry spell ended. The long rainy days started and the outpatient department was crowded daily with children and babies suffering from bronchitis and pneumonia. It was difficult to estimate how many survived – there was no ward to nurse them in and some never returned after the first treatment. That Saturday the patients were very many and Dr Joseph, Matron Jack and Sister Cocks worked conscientiously till dusk. Wearily, they walked home praying that Sunday would bring with it God's blessing. Then Matron Jack remembered a letter that her mother had written to her. She had read it, and left it in the drawer in her office – she needed it to reply to her mother at night when all was quiet.

As she walked back to the outpatients' department, she saw four men carrying a thing that looked like a stretcher. She could not be sure. She gave them another long look. Yes, she was right. Following closely in the wake of the four men was a woman wearing a cloth round her waist. She must have been weeping, for she held her head with both hands as if it was too heavy for the neck. Matron Jack took her eyes away from the pall-bearers. The hospital had been closed for a month. If they did not know that, then they would never know anything. She entered her office, took the letter and then hurried home.

She was too exhausted to argue with the local people, whose language she could not understand. She removed her white hospital cap and sat on a basket chair facing a strip of garden with a blanket of the colourful flowers that had just come out with the first rains. Their beauty pacified her tumbled heart. She loved flowers. Africa was a land of startling beauty. There was no question about that. Yet at the back of her mind she knew that there was something wicked about Africa that scared her. Its thunders were louder, its nights had a ghostly kind of darkness and its people suffered from all kinds of scourges. She looked up and saw the watchman, Okutima, walking towards her. She stiffened, and stared at him with wide eyes. She got up stiffly and walked towards the watchman.

"*Nini,* Okutima?" she asked the watchman nervously.

"*Kuja,*" the watchman beckoned at her, and without waiting he rushed back to the hospital. Matron Jack felt irritated. She hated the way Okutima simply told her 'Come' without saying what they wanted her for. Issaca was on duty and it was time they left her alone to rest. As she passed the theatre, she saw a group of people standing near the women's ward. She moved faster, and her eyes caught the head of Issaca. Then she saw Norman and other male nurses from the men's ward, What could it be? She wriggled her way through the group.

"What is it? Who is there, Issaca? Who?"

But instead of replying, Issaca pulled the blanket off the face of a young woman who lay curled up on the stretcher, dying. The Matron took the head of the girl in both hands and turned it upwards, and she let it drop on its side as if it was a hot brick which scalded her hands. "But, but," she stammered. "But it's Monica, Issaca, it's my Monica. What have they done to my Monica?"

Matron Jack was introduced to the woman with a cloth tied round the waist. She was Monica Adhiambo's mother. She turned to her and grabbed her carelessly by the arm.

"What have you done to my Monica?"

The woman did not reply and the workmen and the relatives of the dying girl stood looking somewhat puzzled by the Matron's love for Monica. She wept publicly and the workmen who had never seen a European cry also started to sob loudly.

On the orders of Matron Jack the annex to the women's ward was opened and a bed prepared for Monica Adhiambo. Dr Joseph was called in. When he examined the patient, he found that she was barely conscious. Matron Jack put a bedpan under her and whispered to her to strain down and open her bowels. She passed what looked like fresh blood from a bleeding vein. Dr Joseph gasped at the sight of the specimen. It must be advanced dysentry or an acute case of typhoid. Norman Olando, the pathologist, was there and examined the specimen immediately. Within a few hours it was clear that Monica was suffering from advanced amoebic dysentry. The doctor told the parents that the girl might not live. Her intestines were all lacerated and her whole body had lost too much of the salt and water that was vital for life. Adhiambo's father stood silent with the other pall-bearers. They had earlier on told Dr Joseph that Adhiambo had refused to come to the hospital.

The evening was far spent. Matron Jack sat at the bedside of the patient reading her Bible. Suddenly she stopped reading and closed the book, keeping one finger on the page she was reading. Big blocks of tears rolled from her eyes and she turned her head slowly away from Adhiambo's mother so as not alarm her. All these weeks she had hoped that one day Monica, and her friends would change their minds and return to the hospital. Everybody at the hospital knew that Monica Adhiambo did not nurse grievances. She was frank, and when annoyed she simply exploded. But it was the kind of explosion that always ended with a laugh. The workmen loved her because she was kind. If tea and boiled bananas were left over from the women's ward, she would rush with them to the workmen and tease them saying, "You greedy things! You always have an eye on my jug of tea." And she would add amidst the men's laughter – "If the old white witch sees me and sacks me, I will haunt the whole lot of you."

Her kindness, efficiency and courage had endeared her to all groups at the hospital. The workmen nicknamed her 'the daughter of the old white witch'; the male members of staff called her 'the child of a donkey', because she was strong; and to her fellow nurses she was always Mony'. Even Dr Joseph and Matron Jack agreed that Adhiambo was a very gifted child, a born leader.

Her thoughts turned from the past and she glanced at Monica again – now mere bones. She must have been badly sick for two weeks at least. Her skin was dry and ashen, her eyes sunken, and what used to be thick moist lips were dried up and cracked. There was no trace of life on her face and the determined mouth that used to twitch when she was annoyed now lay limp and withdrawn to her cheek-bones. The only sign of life was the big jugular vein which pulsated weakly at the pit of her neck. Matron glanced at Adhiambo's mother sitting on a stool at the corner. She was slumbering a little and the long white marks left on her face by the dry tears were still visible – so were the large dark marks under her eyelids which were the signs of many nights of sleeplessness.

"Yes, this is Africa," the white woman said to herself – "Mother watching and waiting in terror for the inevitable end."

Forty-eight hours passed and Monica showed no signs of response to the salty saline that had been put to drip through her veins to replace the water which she lost through diarrhoea. The doctor explained that the saline had been removed because her veins were collapsed and the saline no longer went in, but leaked onto the muscles outside the veins, causing oedema. But it was clear that most of his listeners did not understand the strange jargon. Throughout that morning the workmen, one by one, walked in, bowed their heads close to Monica's bed and walked away. Some wept, many were tongue-tied. Rev Odhuno made a cross with holy water on Monica's forehead – the best parting gift that a dying Christian can receive. Any lingering hopes were dashed by Dr Joseph's laconic announcement that, "it is just a matter of hours".

Then it started to pour with rain, and there was thunder and lightning. Monica's mother moved nearer and knelt beside her daughter. Matron Jack moved away for her. Awiti knew that the flash and thunder had come to take away the spirit of her daughter. She fingered Monica's hands like a toy and then left them to drop on the bed. Then she buried her head in her clothes and sobbed aloud. The relatives and hospital staff who were sheltering in the room nearby rushed in, but Matron Jack waved them away.

Then, as the rain subsided, Monica gradually opened her eyes. Matron beckoned the dying girl's mother. The two looked at each other without uttering a word. Only the tears on their eyes betrayed their thoughts. When Monica saw Matron Jack and Dr Joseph, she wept bitterly. She now realised that her mother had brought her to the hospital against her wish. When she stopped weeping she opened her eyes wide, and then whispered to her mother, "Return to Father – I am staying with the Old White Witch."

The Bamboo Hut

The setting sun was ablaze, and its angry rays coloured the waters on Lake Victoria. Mboga's heart beat fast. He had never seen the disc of the setting sun look so big and ominous. He moved towards the foot of the sacred Hill of Ramogi where his forefathers had from time immemorial worshipped God and pleaded with the ancestors.

For many years Mboga had beseeched Ramogi, the ancestor of the Luo people, to intercede on his behalf for a son, an heir to the headed stool of the Kadibo people. He had decided to make one final plea on this sacred spot. He spat in the direction of the setting sun, and then prayed.

> God of Ramogi and God of Podho
> You led us from distant lands,
> And protected us against all our enemies.
> You gave us land and other possessions,
> Let the name of Ramogi continue,
> Let us multiply and expand in all directions,
> People call me Mboga the Mighty, the handsome ruler,
> Father of the clan.
> What is a mighty ruler without a son?
> What is a father without an heir?

Darkness was falling when Mboga reached home. In the inner compound of his homestead, his 'numerous daughters' as he always referred to them, were busy helping their mothers prepare the evening meal. And although he loved all his sixteen daughters, they were like the birds of the air who, at the appropriate season, migrate to other lands. Who would comfort and succour him in old age?

The drizzle that had started in the evening continued up to the early hours of the next day. The children stayed in their mothers' huts. Agiso took a red sweet potato from a basket and buried it in the cow-dung fire. She added a handful of dry cow-dung to the fire, and then turned to Achieng her mother.

"Mama – why can't we live in the bamboo hut? It is clean, cosy, cool and beautiful. Please ask Baba if we can move into it," she said appealingly.

"But our hut is one of the best in the compound, my child."

"I know that, Mama, but it can't beat the bamboo hut. Our hut has no inner chamber and we have no bamboo beds or beaded stools."

Agiso took a wooden poker and turned the potato over.

"Right, Mama," she said, throwing the poker down. "If you are afraid of the chief, I will ask him myself. I am not afraid."

The bamboo hut stood next to the chief's large hut. It looked beautiful in the morning drizzle. Agiso's mother took her eyes away from it. She was expecting her second baby after an interval of nearly seven years. She knew it would be a girl. The chief, who had nine wives, had promised the bamboo hut to whoever bore him a son, an heir to the beaded stool.

Two months after Mboga's visit to the sacred hill, Achieng gave birth while she was out at the well – it was a baby girl.' The long-nursed desire for a son turned her heart against the baby, and she wept bitterly. "How do I break this sad news to my husband? Will the chief bear the thought of another girl? No, no, no. Let my mouth remain sealed for ever – the ancestors have wronged me." But Achiengs weeping was interrupted by a sharp pain that stabbed her belly and her back. It was like one of those miracles that occur only once in a while. Achieng gave birth again – it was a boy!

The riverbank was still deserted as most women did not fetch water at midday. Everything was so quiet, apart from a few frogs who seemed to be rejoicing with her. She felt very tired, and for a few minutes different passions played a wild dance within her. Love, hatred, anger and happiness crossed and intermingled. The chief had waited for a son for over twelve years. Let the chief have only one child, a son, so that he might see the fulfilment of his life's dream. Achieng made up her mind. She made a grass basket and lined it with leaves – there she laid Apiyo and hid the basket near the well. She gave her a long, rime and last look, and then ran a finger over her face, hair, lips and delicate fingers. She then walked home with her baby boy, and slipped into her hut unnoticed while people were having their midday meal.

The important news was conveyed to Chief Mboga by his older wife while he was resting in his hut.

"God of Ramogi has covered the nakedness of the lather of the people. Achieng has given birth to a baby boy"

Mboga looked at his wife unbelievingly. A joyous smile played on his lips, and then disappeared, leaving only muscles twitching at the corners of his mouth. He eyed his wife and then got up to go to Achiengs hut. But his elder wife barred his way.

"The great chief should not be over-powered by motion. Achieng is under the care of women for four days. Only then can the great chief see his beloved son."

Mboga moved a few steps backwards and sat on his stool. "All right, tell Achieng that I have received the news." Then the Chief's drum boomed out to announce the birth of a new baby. This time it boomed out four times instead of the usual three for a girl, and the family rejoiced. Envy mixed with bitterness in the minds of Achiengs co-wives, but they did not show it. A sheep was slaughtered for the delivered mother and all good things were showered upon her.

Chief Mboga never laughed or shed tears in public, but on the fourth day when he held his son at a naming ceremony, his close relatives saw big lumps of tears rolling down his cheeks as he called out the name of the boy.

"You will be called 'Owiny' after the second son of Ramogi. You will live long, and in my old age you will hold the staff of Ramogi in your right hand to rule your people!" Then the chief's beaded staff was placed in Owiny's right hand and the chief's ornamental bracelet put on his wrist.

On that day, Achieng and Agiso, her daughter, moved to the bamboo hut. There, they were to bring up Owiny, heir to Mboga's beaded stool. The chief offered numerous thanks-giving sacrifices at the foot of the sacred hill. His prayers always ended with the refrain:

"Now I know you did indeed choose me to be a ruler among these people. You have given me a son."

Amid all the revelry, Achieng maintained a most singular gravity. She felt as if something in her heart were breaking. She couldn't go on like this any longer. But what was to be done? Should she look for her daughter? No, she couldn't do anything like that. Could she tell her husband the truth – but how?

She went to the well on the sixth day to bathe herself after confinement: She walked hurriedly past the place where she had abandoned her daughter Apiyo. There was nothing on the spot to betray her, and the long grass stood erect as though nothing had ever rested on it. As she trudged along on her way home, Achieng had many thoughts, confused thoughts, but thoughts nevertheless, and even visions, about her lost daughter.

She saw an old withered woman pick up her daughter by the well. She saw her perform a kind of witches' dance round the basket, more carrying it away. The mute followed by the old woman was towards the no-man's land lying between the Kadibo folk and their enemies. She then saw her daughter being thrown away in this forest, which was known to be infested with wild animals.

Unconsciously, she yelled! Her heart began to beat and a sudden moisture wetted the middle of her palms. Was it true? "No, no, no!" she replied.

Years slipped by, but Achiengs distraught mind showed no signs of improvement. It was a life of visions and depression in the daytime, and of nightmares at night. Neither her privileged position among the chief's wives nor the future prospect for her son were adequate to fill the acute emptiness she felt in her heart.

Owiny grew up into a fine, strong man, with the usual characteristics of single children − sulky, headstrong and independent. One afternoon, as the chief was on one of his regular walks to the sacred hill, he encountered a group of young women carrying loads of firewood. The girls left the path and hid behind the long bushes to let the chief pass. But one girl put her bundle down and stood waiting. When the chief got close to her, she bowed her head and greeted him.

"Peace be with you, great chief."

"Peace, my child," said the chief, who was obviously moved by the courage of this young girl.

"Are you not afraid of the chief like your sisters?" the chief teased her.

"No. It is my lucky day to meet the kind chief."

Then she put the bundle on her head and walked away.

That night Mboga called his son and told him about the young woman.

"She is the daughter of Owuor Chilo the clan elder of Usigu. She is visiting her aunt here. Try and see her tomorrow. If you like her, we will approach her parents. She should make a good wife."

Owiny was curious to meet the young lady whose personality had impressed the chief so much. He kept watch on her movements; and when a messenger informed him that the girl and her friends had been seen swimming in the river Odundu, he immediately rushed to the scene.

At the river half a dozen young women were swimming and shouting at one another. One of the older girls saw Owiny first, and rushed out of the water yelling, "The chief's son! The chief's son!"

The girls, taken unaware, scrambled out of the water and hid behind the nearest bushes. But the girl who obviously looked younger than the others continued to swim, undisturbed. Owiny moved closer to her.

"Why aren't you afraid of the son of the chief?" he asked her, jokingly.

The girl was not bashful. She looked knowingly at him, raised her head a little and, concealing her breasts, said, "Because the son of the chief does not respect ladies' privacy."

"I was on my way to the hills to hunt, when I heard some shrieking noises, I therefore came to check."

"Right," she said with finality, as she dived in and out. "Now that you know who were shrieking, you can continue with your journey."

Owiny stood there puzzled. This foolhardy girl was not from his clan – her accent was foreign. She could be the girl the chief had told him about.

"Can't you come out and give your friends their loin cloths? I didn't mean to be rude to them."

"It would be better it you left us alone, we are still swimming."

"No," Owiny said firmly. "I want to talk to all of you about the coming festival of the chief."

"All right." she said. "Throw me my loin cloth – it is the beaded one?"

Owiny was shocked by the girl's natural air of importance. He never took orders from anyone, let alone any woman – he was always waited upon. He swallowed his pride and threw her the beaded loin cloth. The girl wrapped her loin cloth round her waist and emerged from the water unafraid. She grabbed the other loin cloths in her arm and handed them to her friends behind the bushes.

Owiny felt warm and uncomfortable where he stood. For the first time in his life he was unsure of himself. He took a close look at the girl – she was much older than the chief had suggested. Her long slender legs would fill up with maturity. Her fingers were long and graceful; and she had a straight back: and flat lovable belly. Her breasts were still young and stood erect like wooden carvings on her chest.

Her skin dotted with water was the colour of the rising sun. As Owiny looked at her, she reminded him of Arosi, the legendary and beautiful goddess of the sea. They exchanged a few words and she told Owiny that her name was Awiti.

That evening Owiny was in a melancholy mood. A newly discovered fire was burning in his heart. He reported to his father that he had seen the girl and that he liked her very much.

In those days the marriage preliminaries for the son of a chief were conducted with proper punctilio. The chief therefore sent out messengers to investigate the girl's background. Gossip had reached Achieng that her would-be daughter-in-law had no equal for beauty in all Luoland. She had, moreover, been brought up with great care and was diligent.

The messengers returned with red dust on their feet and empty bellies. On seeing them, Chief Mboga went to his hut to receive the news.

They told him:

"The family of Owuor Chilo did not deal with us kindly when we inquired about the girl. It seemed that a word had reached them that the young man, your son, may be seeking her hand in marriage. They insisted that Awiti was too young that they should be given time. But we pressed them. We had seen the girl – she is beautiful and ripe for marriage. The family then conferred among themselves outside, and when they joined us, they told us that Awiti may not wish to marry the chief's son."

The messenger who was speaking looked at the chief anxiously and moistened his dry lips.

"Go on," the chief roared aggressively.

He looked past them so that they could not notice the angry frown which distorted his face.

"They said, great chief, that it is impossible." Mboga's fame was not confined to his clan alone. Who was Owuor Chilo whose daughter could reject the offer of the son of the chief?

"Go on," he repeated.

"We were not satisfied with the excuses given, so we called at a neighbouring village and enquired circumspectly about the girl. We were told that Awiti has no parents. She was found abandoned by the well by Owuor's elder wife who adopted her."

The messenger cleared his throat, and mopped away a mushroom of sweat from his forehead.

The air suddenly became still and suffocating, as Chief Mboga discharged his messengers. He knocked his pipe on a wooden log nearby to empty the dead ashes. Owiny's new hut caught his eye. Mboga knew that his son would not accept the news. But a chief's son could not marry a non-entity, a woman of unknown parentage.

That evening when the restless cows had been milked and the tired children sat round the fire by their mothers waiting for the evening meal Owiny was summoned to the chief's hut. Mboga broke the sad news to his son.

"My son, you cannot marry Chile's daughter. She was abandoned as a baby by the well – the wife of Chilo found her and brought her up."

Mboga sucked his pipe and then spat on the hard-beaten floor.

"As the future ruler of the land you cannot marry a woman whose background is a mystery."

Owiny tightened his buttocks on the oily stool he was sitting on. He wanted to rise and leave the chief's hut, but he fell back. Breath had gone out of him and he felt dizzy. As he recovered from the shock, he had a hazy vision of Awiti – he saw her beautiful figure and her provocative breasts. The fire revived in him. He must tell his father the truth.

"Father let me take her to be my wife. I love her. I want to live with her. I ..."

Tears choked Owiny and he could not complete the sentence.

"No, my son," the chief said. "She is not good enough for our home – the ancestors would be displeased. We shall find you a suitable woman."

Owiny got up unexpectedly, paced up and down the room and then turned sharply to face his father.

"Will the great chief change his mind and allow me to marry the woman I desire?"

Mboga gripped the ruling staff tightly.

"No," he thundered and his voice rang in the still night. Owiny stood before his father for a while before he spoke gravely.

"Great chief, you will not see my face again. I have chosen the daughter of Chilo – you can keep your beaded stool."

Without waiting for his father's reply, Owiny left. He shut himself up in his hut – he wished to blot the whole world out of his sight. What was he to do? Commit suicide? No, he must live to marry Awiti. Run away! But to where?

The dismay in the homestead, when the news became known may well be imagined. But all the uncles, aunts and other relatives agreed with the chief that Awiti would not make a suitable wife for Mboga's son. Only Achieng, Owiny's mother, knew the truth. Was she to die with this secret? Her son's life was at stake – why not face the chief and tell him the truth? She might ruin his life; but he was old enough to die. Her son had all his life before him. She made up her mind – she must say it.

She went to the chief's hut and fell at his feet weeping.

"She is my daughter. Awiti is the daughter of the great chief, and twin sister to Owiny, your son. I abandoned her by the well because I wanted to give you nothing but a son."

Mboga sat still and the hairs on his skin stood erect like those of a frightened cat. The scene on the path from the sawed hill when Awiti greeted him by the roadside came to his mind. Yes, her face resembled that of his son. Mboga looked past his wife into the dark night. Only a few hours more and it would be sunrise, then the whole land would know the truth. He knew his people were going to persuade him to send Achieng away. She had thrown away her new born baby, she had angered the ancestors, she was not worthy of being a chief's wife.

But Mboga made up his mind. No one was going to take Achieng from him. She was the centre of his life. The self doubt that often follows the betrayal of life long trust crept into Mboga's mind. He wondered what other secrets were still hidden in the bosoms of his wives. He lifted Achiengs head from his feet.

"Mother of Awiti, arise. For my sake you have borne a heavy burden for many years. You have denied yourself the pleasure a mother gets from swinging her child. Go and tell your son that he has a very beautiful sister. I shall give him my choicest bull to slaughter and eat with his sister and friends. Let us all rejoice and thank our ancestor Ramogi."

The Hero

"Help, help, help." I yelled.

"The landslide was still burying me, my climbing rope was broken and I had lost touch with the other mountaineers.

"Hel ... p me!"

I gasped and wriggled in great panic. The cruel earth was breaking my bones and squashing me into nothingness.

"Wa ... w!" I yelled again, and covered my head with both hands. A large rock was rolling towards me.

I struggled into a sitting position from the terrible dream. My whole body was wet with perspiration. The end parts of the blanket were very damp, and there was a large patch on the pillow. My eyes moved slowly from side to side, and the empty beds stared at me. All the night nurses had gone on duty except me. I was late. I slipped the uniform and cap on my sweaty body and took a short-cut through the chapel. The candles on the altar were almost out and the large silver crucifix behind a jar of roses looked tampered with. My heart leapt. There must be some sad news awaiting me. Perhaps the matron had received a telegram conveying some terrible news, perhaps about a dead relative, from home. I slipped out of the chapel on to the main road that ran through the hospital. There were more people standing around the hospital wards than usual. The matron's office came into view, the windows were open, and the pale light emitted through the curtains had turned golden with dusk. My knees suddenly weakened and for a while I forgot about my lateness and almost burst into tears. Avoiding the matron's cat-like eyes, I made one desperate step through the swing door into the ward.

As I tip-toed towards the duty room, I saw four doctors standing facing room twelve. My thoughts shifted from the telegram and my people at home. Someone very important had been admitted. Perhaps Dr Harris, the hospital superintendent, was very sick, for I had never seen so many doctors together before. I threw my bag and cap in the corner and, as I fumbled for the day's report, my eyes caught something on the blue case-sheet at the far end of the table. I picked up the papers with trembling hands and read on.

'Room 12 Doctor Eric Sserwadda Age 31.
Admitted at 4.30 p.m.
Diagnosis: High fever and numbness of R. Log?
Poliomyelitis!'

For a moment everything went blank, and my heart missed a beat. I turned the case-sheet upside down. But the words were written wherever I looked, on the walls, on the furniture, everywhere. Could it be another Eric? Another doctor with the same name? But no, I had not heard of another doctor Eric Sserwadda, and the one I knew could not be older or younger than 31. But from where could Eric contract polio? From one of his patients, or was he just suffering from a bad attack of malaria? I tiptoed into Room 12 without caring how many doctors and sisters were there. There upon the bed my blurry eyes rested on Eric Sserwadda, my secret idol and hero, the man who had once cured my mother from a rare blood disease which no doctor in Kenya could cure. A cradle had been put over his numb leg to relieve the weight of the bed clothes. His striped red pyjamas made him look ghastly pale. A mushroom of perspiration stood on his dehydrated face and his thin dry lips were pressed together. His eyes were open, but they stared blankly into space as though they could not focus.

I took a step towards the bed. Suddenly I became aware of Sister Moore and Sister Hudson wearing isolation gowns. Their looks were enough to warn me that I had no isolation gown. I fixed my eyes on my hero again and, for a moment, I thought he saw me. He had moved as if to make a gesture with his left hand, but it fell back on the pillow as though he had lost power to control it. I could not stay there a minute longer – the long heaves and the gasps threatened to choke me, and bursting into tears before a patient, I knew, would earn severe disciplinary action from the matron herself. As I tip-toed out of the room, the frightening grip on my shoulders made me swing round, and I came face to face, with Jerudine. Her grip tightened accusingly.

"Tell them to save him, tell them please. He promised me everlasting freedom and happiness. They have to save him. Please tell ... them ..."

She slipped back into the room leaving me there stock-still. Somebody was ringing the bell but I sneaked out on to the verandah facing Mengo Hill. The sun had disappeared completely now, but its golden reflections shone through the hovering clouds and glowed with mellow light between the delicate banana leaves. I let tears spill out from my bulging eyes and they spilt out fast. The huge mango tree near the incinerator was heavy with young green mangoes; two dropped down, and my eyes chased them as they rolled a few inches, before nestling in the grass.

The little rusty tin-roofed huts looked morose but at the same time confident as though they knew something I did not. Vague episodes in Eric Sserwadda's life came to mind. How he had struggled for education, his choice to be a doctor, and now how his people had crowned him a hero when he returned from overseas loaded with degrees. No, it had to be malaria and not polio. My thoughts turned to Jerudine – did she feel the weight her husband was carrying as the only African consultant in the whole land? Did she appreciate what her man's high position meant to a people whose main aspiration was to govern themselves? In him, the country had moved a big step forward towards capturing back the land that belonged to them by right. But even if Jerudine took her husband's position for granted, surely she must also have suspected that so many of us nurses worshipped him secretly. Everything about Eric was immaculate, and he was for us a perfect image of what any woman would want to see in a man. To us whom he knew by name, we were a class apart.

By 12.30 a.m. Dr Sserwadda showed signs of deterioration and he was having difficulty in breathing. Even I who had up till now refused to accept the diagnosis had no choice but to do so. The three specialists looking after him consulted one another and decided to move him to Mulago Hospital. There his breathing could be helped by an iron lung. As we lowered him on to the stretcher, he gave a weak moan which cut me deep to the heart. I looked into his eyes searchingly, but he did not seem to recognise me. Near the ambulance, I squeezed Jerudine's hand and whispered:

"God will spare him, Jerudine, I can feel it." The ambulance had long sped away but none of us seemed to be in a hurry to return to the warmth inside, nor were we conscious of the chill caused by the falling dew. The moon shone dimly and the shadows looked ghostly thin and long, and the twigs did not move. The stillness was only broken by the occasional twitter of the crickets, and the sorrowful moan of the night owl. Uncertainty weighed heavy with us as we returned to the ward to wait in prayer. "I know what you feel. Anna, being Jerudine's close friend, but believe me, we all love Dr Sserwadda. See how he has improved conditions for the African workers during the eighteen months he has been here!" The nurse forced a smile as she said it, but evidently without relishing it.

"I would rather not discuss him now; please." I whispered. "Let us pack drums," I suggested, lamely hiding my wet eyes from Nurse Kigundu.

She got up reluctantly and spread a large white sheet on the table while I brought out the swabs and drums from the long cupboard. "Mm," she sighed heavily, as she sat down and pulled a drum before her. "Why should Eric, a doctor and a specialist, catch polio? I mean with all these laymen in the land, why him?"

I kept absolutely quiet as though I could not hear her. I counted ten swabs, tied them up together and packed them.

She ignored my silence.

"I think it's not polio, Anna, it can't be. Isn't polio only a disease of the children? At least that's what my notes say." I held the swabs in my hand.

"Do you want us to pack these drums or talk? Surely we can't do both."

"I'd rather talk." She tossed the swabs on the table.

"I can't concentrate on anything," she groaned.

"I can't even count the swabs."

The telephone rang. We jumped with fright, and Nurse Kigundu's extended hand sent the drum with a mighty crash to the ground.

"Take it," she ordered.

"No." I buried my hand in my apron.

"Take it, please Anna, please," she begged.

"I can't," I sobbed.

I heard her moving to the table, I heard her say, "Hello ... Hello ... Nurse Kigundu speaking."

There was a pause, then she said, "Thanks be to God Almighty, we will keep on praying." Another pause, and then, "Thanks for calling us, Sister, thanks."

She replaced the receiver and stood there for a while looking at me. "He is doing very well according to Sister Jack, his breathing has eased a lot now and he can talk."

The clock on the wall struck 4 a.m. as I whispered secret prayers to God. Jerudine's chalky face crossed my mind and I bit my lips. She had not known what happiness and freedom was till Eric brought her out from South Africa barely a year ago. She was young and was just starting to settle down in her marriage. If anything were to happen to Eric, she would be as good as dead with no re-entry permit to South Africa, and only a handful of friends in her new country.

The weeping morning wind bit hard around my ankles – something assured me that it was going to be well. If he can pull through the night, he will make it definitely. He will be out of danger, the doctors had said so. I would ask matron for permission to go to Mulago Hospital to see his progress for myself, I would go to the house first, and if Jerudine was not there, I could probably play with the baby, or follow her to the hospital.

At 7.30 a.m. I left Nurse Kigundu clearing breakfast trays while I went to clean the sluice-room. I had not been there a minute when I heard the night sister calling out, "Nurse, nurse!"

My heartbeat thudded away painfully as I dabbed my hands on the towel. Sister Mary stood in the corridor with a broad grin on her face. My heartbeat eased, but I did not return her smile. Nurse Kigundu and I reached her at the same time.

"He is dead," Sister Mary stammered. "Doctor Eric Sserwadda died at 4.30 a.m."

I pulled myself together and forced air into my lungs. Nurse Kigundu let out an anguished shriek and flopped on the floor. What I thought was a broad grin, was no grin at all. Sister Mary was crying and her eyes were red and sore. Without another word she hurried away from us to other wards.

That day was long and angry, and I had no desire to see Jerudine or to care for the baby. Weary in body and soul, I joined the other night nurses and we cried together until we had no more tears left, and the evening sunlight filtered through the night-nurses' apartment.

Two long and weary days passed. On the third day, the hero's body was carried to the Kampala City Central Cemetery, at the head of a long funeral cortege. The hearse gave a clear view of the coffin within and its smothering mantle of flowers. Behind it followed a shuffling parade of mourners.

Eric Sserwadda looked merely asleep in the glass coffin. The little facial wrinkles were no longer there; and the thin lips pressed together had an unpronounced message. I could only guess this important message: he had not been prepared for this long journey.

The loud and shrill voices of mourners faded to mere snuffling as the Bishop said, "What has come from dust must return to dust." As the mourners prepared to throw earth into the grave a terrifying female voice yelled, "No, no, no, don't crush his bones he is my only son."

The stillness, the heat and the sorrow became profound and unbearable. On the haggard faces of grief-stricken mourners, streak of sweat and tears mingled and dropped to the ground.

I remembered my dreadful dream: the earth had buried and crushed me into nothingness. Still holding red fresh soil in trembling hands, I pushed my way from the graveside.

Tekayo

The period of short rains was just starting in a semi-arid part of the Sudan. The early morning mist had cleared and faint blue smoke rose from the ground as the hot sun touched the surface of the wet earth.

"People, in the underworld are cooking.

People in the underworld are cooking!"

The children shouted, as they pelted one another with wet sand.

"Come on, Opija," Tekayo shouted to his son. "Give me a hand, I must get the cows to the rivers before it is too hot."

Opija hit his younger brother with his last handful of sand, and then ran to help his father. The cows were soon out of the village and Tekayo picked up the leather pouch containing his lunch and followed them.

They had not gone far from home when Tekayo saw an eagle flying above his head with a large piece of meat in its claws. The eagle was flying low searching for a suitable spot to have its meal. Tekayo promptly threw his stick at the bird. He hit the meat and it dropped to the ground. It was a large piece of liver, and fresh blood was still oozing from it. Tekayo nearly threw the meat away, but he changed his mind. What was the use of robbing the eagle of its food only to throw it away? The meat looked good: it would supplement his vegetable lunch wonderfully. He wrapped the meat in a leaf and pushed it into his pouch.

They reached a place where there was plenty of grass. Tekayo allowed the cows to graze while he sat under an Ober tree watching the sky. It was not yet lunch time, but Tekayo could not wait. The desire to taste that meat was burning within him. He took out the meat and roasted it on a log fire under the Ober tree. When the meat was cooked he ate it greedily with millet bread which his wife had made the previous night.

"My! What delicious meat?" Tekayo exclaimed. He licked the fat juice that stained his fingers, and longed for a little more. He threw away the bitter herbs that were the rest of his lunch. The meat was so good, and the herbs would merely spoil its taste.

The sun was getting very hot; but the cows showed no desire to go to the river to drink. One by one they lay down in the shade, chewing the cud. Tekayo also became overpowered by the afternoon heat. He rested against the trunk and slept.

While asleep, Tekayo had a dream. He was sitting before a log fire roasting a large, piece of liver like the one he had eaten earlier. His mouth watered as he watched rich fat from the roasting meat dropping into the fire. He could not wait, and although the meat was not completely done, he removed it from the fire and cut it up with his hunting knife. But just as he was about to take the first bite, he woke up.

Tekayo looked around him, wondering what had happened to the meat! Could it be that he was dreaming? "No, no, no," he cried. "It was too vivid to be a dream!" He sat upright and had another look around, as if by some miracle he might see a piece of liver roasting on the log fire beside him. But there was nothing. All he saw were large roots of the old tree protruding above the earth's surface like sweet potatoes in the sandy soil.

The cattle had wandered a long way off. Tekayo got up and followed them. They reached the river bank, and the thirsty cows ran to the river. While the cows drank, Tekayo sat on a white stone cooling his feet and gazing lazily at the swollen river as it flowed mightily towards the plain.

Beyond the river stood the great 'Ghost Jungle'. A strong desire for the rich meat came back to Tekayo, and he whispered, "The animal with that delicious liver must surely be in that jungle." He sat there for a while, thinking. The temptation to start hunting for the animal nagged him. But he managed to suppress it. The afternoon was far spent and they were a long way from home.

The next morning Tekayo left home earlier than usual. When his wife begged him to wait for his lunch, he refused. He hurried from home, taking his hunting spears with him.

Tekayo made it impossible for the cows to graze. He rushed them along, lashing at any cow that lingered in one spot for long. They reached the edge of the 'Ghost Jungle' and there he left the cows grazing unattended.

Tekayo could not see any path or track leading into the 'Ghost Jungle'. The whole place was a mass of thick bush and long grass covered with the morning dew. And except for the sounds of mating, there was a weird silence in the jungle that frightened him. But the vehement desire within him blindly drove him on, through the thick wet grass.

After walking for some time, he stood and listened. Something was racing towards him. He turned round to look, and sure enough a big impala was running frantically towards him. Warm blood rushed through Tekayo's body, and he raised his spear to kill the animal. But the spear never landed – He came face to face with a big leopardess that was chasing the impala. The leopardess roared at Tekayo several times challenging him, as it were, to a duel. But Tekayo looked away, clutching the spear in his trembling hand. There was no one to fight and the beast went away after her prey. "What a bad start," Tekayo said slowly and quietly when his heart beat normally again. "That wild cat will not leave me alone now."

He started to walk back towards the plain, following the track he had made. The roaring leopardess had taken the life out of him.

He saw another track that cut across the forest. He hesitated a little, and then decided to follow it, leaving his own. The track got bigger and bigger, and without any warning Tekayo suddenly came upon a baby wildebeeste which was following a large flock grazing at the foot of a hill. He killed it without any difficulty. He skinned the animal and extracted its liver, leaving the rest of the carcass there.

Tekayo returned to the herd, and he sat down to roast the meal on a log fire. When the meat was cooked he took a bite and chewed it hurriedly. But he did not swallow it: he spat it all out! The liver was as bitter as the strong green herbs given to constipated children. The back of his tongue was stinging as if it had been burned. Tekayo threw the rest of the meat away and took his cows home.

He arrived home tired and disappointed; and when his young wife set food before him, he refused to eat. He pretended that he had stomachache and did not feel like eating. That night Tekayo was depressed and in low spirits. He did not even desire his young wife who slept by his side. At dawn the young wife returned to her hut disappointed, wondering why the old man had not desired her. The doors of all the huts were still closed when Tekayo looked out through his door. A cold east wind hit his face, and he quickly shut himself in again.

It was getting rather late and the calves were calling. But it was pouring with rain so much that he could not start milking. He sat on the hard bed looking at the dead ashes in the fire-place. He longed to get out to start hunting.

When the rain stopped, Tekayo milked the cows in a great hurry. Then he picked up the lunch that had been left near his hut for him, and left the village. His disappointed wife of the previous night watched him till he disappeared at the gate.

When he reached the 'Ghost Jungle' it was drizzling again. The forest looked so lonely and wet. He left the cows grazing as usual, and entered the bush, stealing his way through the dripping leaves. He turned to the left to avoid the thick part of the jungle. Luck was with him. He spotted a family of antelopes grazing not far from him. He crawled on his knees till he was quite close to them, and then threw his spear killing one animal instantly. After skinning it, he extracted its liver, and also took some delicate parts for the family.

When he sat down under the tree to roast the meat, Tekayo was quite sure that he had been successful. But when he tasted the meat, he shook his head. The meat was tender, but it was not what he was looking for.

They reached the river bank. The cows continued to graze after drinking, and Tekayo, without realising it, wandered a long way from his herd, still determined to discover the owner of that wonderful liver. When he suddenly looked round, the herd was nowhere to be seen. The sun was sinking behind Mount Pajulu, and Tekayo started to run, looking for his cows.

The cows, heavy with milk, had gone home without Tekayo. For one day when Tekayo's children got lost in the forest, the cows had gone home without them, following the old track they knew well. On that day the whole village came out in search of the children in fear that the wild animals might harm them.

It was getting dark when Tekayo arrived home. They started to milk and Odipo remarked, "Why, father, you are late coming home today."

"It is true," lied Tekayo thoughtfully. "See that black bull there? He went to another herd across the river. I didn't miss him until it was time to come home. One of these days we shall have to castrate him – he is such a nuisance."

They milked in silence until one of the little girls came to fetch some milk for preparing vegetables.

At supper time the male members of the family sat around the log fire waiting and talking. One by one, baskets of millet meal and earthen dishes of meat and vegetables arrived from different huts. There was fish, dried meat, fried white ant, and herbs. A little food was thrown to the ground, to the ancestors, and then they started eating. They compared and contrasted the deliciousness of the various dishes they were having. But Tekayo kept quiet. All the food he tasted that evening was bitter as bile.

When the meal was over, the adults told stories of war and the clans to the children, who listened attentively. But Tekayo was not with them: he was not listening. He watched the smoky clouds as they raced across the sky.

"Behind those clouds, behind those clouds, rests Okenyu, my great-grandfather. Please! Please!" Tekayo beseeched him. "Please, father, take this longing away from me. Give me back my manhood that I may desire my wives. For what is a man without this desire!"

A large cloud covered the moon giving the earth temporary darkness. Tears stung Tekayo's eyes, and he dismissed the family to sleep. As he entered his own hut, a woman was throwing small logs on the fire.

He offered many secret prayers to the departed spirits, but the craving for the mysterious liver never left him. Day after day he left home in the morning, taking his cows with him. And on reaching the jungle, he left them unattended while he hunted. The rough and disappointed life that he led soon became apparent to the family. He suddenly became old and disinterested in life. He had nothing to tell his sons around the evening fire, and he did not desire his wives. The sons of Tekayo went to Lakech and told her, "Mother, speak to father, he is sick. He does not talk to us, and he does not eat. We don't know how to approach him."

Though Lakech had passed the age of child-bearing and no longer went to Tekayo's hut at night, she was his first wife, and he loved her. She therefore went and asked him, "Man, what ails you?" Tekayo looked at Lakech, but he could not look into her eyes.

He looked at her long neck, and instead of answering her question he asked her, "Would you like to get free from those heavy brass rings around your neck?"

"Why?" Lakech asked, surprised.

"Because they look so tight."

"But they are not tight," Lakech said softly. "I would feel naked without them."

And Tekayo looked away from his wife. He was longing to tell Lakech everything, and to share with her this maddening craving that was tearing his body to pieces. But he checked himself. Lakech must not know: she would not understand. Then he lied to her. "It is my old indigestion. I have had it for weeks now. It will soon pass."

A mocking smile played on Lakech's lips, and Tekayo knew that she was not convinced. Some visitors arrived, and Lakech, left her husband.

Tekayo hunted for many months, but he did not succeed in finding the animal with the delicious liver.

One night, as he lay awake, he asked himself where else he could hunt. And what animal would he be looking for? He had killed all the different animals in the 'Ghost Jungle'. He had risked his life when he killed and ate the liver of a lion, a leopard and a hyena, all of which were tabooed by his clan.

A little sleep came to Tekayo's heavy eyes and he was grateful. But then Apii stood beside his bed calling: "Grandpa, Grandpa, it is me." Tekayo sat up, but the little girl was not there. He went back to sleep again. And Apii was there calling him: "Can't you hear me Grandpa?"

Tekayo woke up a second time, but nobody was there. He lay down without closing his eyes. Again the child's fingers touched his drooping hand, and the playful voice of a child tickled the skin of the old man. Tekayo sat up a third time, and looked round the room. But he was alone. The cock crew a third time, and it was morning.

And Lakech died without knowing her husband's secret, and was buried in the middle of the village, being the first wife.

Tekayo sat at his wife's grave morning and evening for a long time, and his grief for her appeased his hunger for the unknown animal's liver. He wept, but peacefully, as if his craving for the liver was buried with his wife.

It was during this time of grief that Tekayo decided never to go hunting again. He sat at home and looked after his many grandchildren, while the younger members of the family went out to work daily in the fields.

And then one day as Tekayo sat warming himself in the early morning sun near the granary, he felt slightly sick from the smell of grain sprouting inside the dark store. The shouting and singing of his grandchildren attracted his attention. As he watched them playing, the craving for the liver of the unknown animal returned powerfully to him.

Now among the children playing was a pretty little girl called Apii, the daughter of Tekayo's eldest son. Tekayo, sent the other children away to play, and as they were going, he called Apii and told her, "Come my little one, run to your mother's hut and bring me a calabash of water."

Apii ran to her mother's hut to get water for her grandfather. And while she was fumbling in a dark corner of the house looking for a clean calabash, strong hands gripped her neck and strangled her. She gave a weak cry as she struggled for the breath of life. But it was too much for her.

Her eyes closed in everlasting sleep, never to see the beauty of the shining moon again.

The limp body of the child slipped from Tekayo's hands and fell on the floor with a thud. He looked at the body at his feet and felt sick and faint. His ears were buzzing. He picked up the body, and as he staggered out with it, the air seemed black, and the birds of the air screamed onminously at him. But Tekayo had to eat his meal. He buried the body of Apii in a nearby anthill in a shallow grave. The other children were still playing in the field when Tekayo returned with the liver in his bag. He roasted it in his hut hastily and ate it greedily. And alas! It was what he had been looking for for many years. He sat lazily resting his back on the granary, belching and picking his teeth. The hungry children, back from their play in the fields, sat in the shade eating sweet potatoes and drinking sour milk.

The older people came back in the evening, and the children ran to meet their parents. But Apii was not among them. In great desperation they asked the grandfather about the child. But Tekayo replied, "Ask the children – they should know where Apii is. They were playing together in the fields."

It was already pitch dark. Apii's younger brothers and sisters sat in front of the fire weeping with their mother. It was then that they remembered their grandfather sending Apii to fetch water for him. The desperate parents repeated this information to the old man, asking him if Apii had brought water for him that morning.

"She did," Tekayo replied, "and then ran away after the others. I watched her go with my own eyes. When they came back, I was asleep."

The grief-stricken family sat near the fireplace, their heads in their hands. They neither ate nor drank. Outside the little crickets sang in chorus as if they had a secret to tell.

For many days Apii's parents looked for their child, searching every corner and every nook. But there was no trace of her. Apii was gone. Months went by, and people talked no more about the disappearance of Apii. Only her mother thought of her. She did not lose hope of finding her child alive one day.

Tekayo forgot his deed. And when he killed a second child in the same way to satisfy his savage appetite, he was not even conscious of what he was doing. And when the worried parents asked the old man about the child, Tekayo wept saying, "How could I know? The children play out in the fields while I stay here at home."

It was after this that Tekayo's sons said among themselves, "Who steals our children? Which animal can it be? Could it be a hyena? Or a leopard? But these animals only hunt at night. Could it be an eagle, because it hunts during the day? But no! Father would have seen the eagle – he would have heard the child screaming." After some thought, Aganda told his brother, "Perhaps it is a malicious animal brought upon us by the evil spirits."

"Then my father is too old to watch the children," put in Osogo.

"Yes, Father is too old, he is in danger," the rest agreed.

And from that time onwards the sons kept watch secretly on the father and the children. They watched for many months, but nothing threatened the man and the children.

The sons were almost giving up the watch. But one day when it was the turn of Apii's father to keep watch, he saw Tekayo sending away the children to play in the field – all except one. He sent this child to fetch him a pipe from his hut. As the child ran to the hut, Tekayo followed him. He clasped the frightened child and dragged him towards the fire. As Tekayo was struggling with the child, a heavy blow landed on his old back. He turned round sharply, his hands still holding the child's neck. He was facing Aganda, his eldest son. The child broke loose from the limp hands of Tekayo and grabbed Aganda's knees as if he had just escaped from the teeth of a crocodile. "Father!" Aganda shouted.

Seeing that the child was not hurt, Aganda pushed him aside saying, "Go to your mother's hut and lie down."

He then got hold of the old man and dragged him towards the little windowless hut built for goats and sheep. As he was being dragged away, the old man kept on crying, *"Atimo ang'o? Atimo ang'o"* (What have I done? What have I done?)

Aganda pushed the old man into the little hut and barred the door behind him, as you would to the animals. He went to the child, who was still sobbing.

The rest of the family returned from the fields, and when Apii's father broke the news to them, they were appalled. The family wore mourning garments and went without food.

'Tho! Tho!' they spat towards the sun which, although setting on them, was rising on the ancestors.

"Great-grandfathers, cleanse us," they all cried. And they lit the biggest fire that had ever been lit in that village. Tekayo's eldest son took the old greasy drum hanging above the fireplace in his father's hut and beat it. The drum throbbed out sorrowful tunes to warn the clan that there was sad news in Tekayo's home. The people who heard the drum left whatever they were doing and ran to Tekayo's village following the sound of the drum. Within a short time the village was teeming with anxious-looking relatives. "What news? What news?" they asked in trembling voices.

"And where is Tekayo?" another old man asked.

"Is he in good health?" asked another.

There was confusion and panic.

"Death of death, who will give us medicine for death? Death knocks at your door, and before you can tell him to come in, he is in the house with you."

"Listen!" Someone touched the old woman who was mourning about death.

Aganda spoke to the people. "Men of my clan. We have not called you here for nothing. Listen to me and let our sorrow be yours. Weep with us! For several months we have been losing our children when we go to work on the fields. Apii, my own child, was the first one to disappear." Sobbing broke out among the women at the mention of the children's names.

"My people," Aganda continued, "the children in this clan get sick and die. But ours disappear unburied. It was our idea to keep watch over our children that we may catch whoever steals them. For months we have been watching secretly. We were almost giving up because we thought it was probably the wrath of our ancestors that was upon us. But today I caught him"

"What man? What man?" the people demanded angrily.

"And from what clan is he?" others asked.

"We must declare war on his clan, we must we must!"

Aganda stopped for a while, and told them in a quavering voice, "The man is in that little hut. The man is no one else but my father."

"*Mayo!*" the women shouted. There was a scuffle and the women and children screamed as if Tekayo was around the fire, and they were afraid of him. But the men kept quiet.

When the commotion died down, an old man asked, "Do you speak the truth, man?"

The son nodded. Men and women now shouted, "Where is the man? Kill him! He is not one of us. He is not one of us. He is an animal!"

There was nothing said outside that Tekayo did not hear. And there in the hut the children he had killed haunted him. He laid his head on the rough wall of the hut and wept.

Outside the hut the angry villagers continued with their

demand, shouting, "Stone him now! Stone him now! Let his blood be upon his own head!"

But one of the old men got up and calmed the people.

"We cannot stone him now. It is the custom of the clan that a wicked man should be stoned in broad daylight, outside the village. We cannot depart from this custom."

"Stone me now, stone me now," Tekayo whispered. "Take me away quickly from this torture and shame. Let me die and be finished with."

Tekayo knew by the angry shouting of the men and the shrill cries of frightened women and children that he was banished from society, nay, from life itself. He fumbled in his leather bag suspended around his waist to find his hunting knife, but it was not there. It had been taken away from him.

The muttering and shouting continued outside. There was weeping too. But Tekayo was now hearing them from afar as if a powerful wave were carrying him further and further away from his people.

At dawn the villagers got up from the fireplace to gather stones from nearby fields. The sun was not up yet, but it was just light enough to see. Everyone in the clan must throw a stone at the murderer. It was bad not to throw a stone, for it was claimed that the murderer's wicked spirit would rest upon the man who did not help to drive him away.

When the first rays of the sun appeared, the villagers had gathered enough stones to cover several bodies. They returned to the village, to fetch Tekayo from the hut, and to lead him to his own garden outside the village. They surrounded the hut and stood in silence, waiting to jeer and spit at him when he came out.

Aganda and three old men tore the papyrus door open and called Tekayo to come out. But there was no reply. They rushed into the hut to drag him out to the people who were now demanding, "Come out, come out!"

At first it was too dark to see. But soon their eyes got used to the darkness. Then they saw the body of Tekayo, hanged on a short rope that he had unwound from the thatched roof.

The men came out shaking their heads. The crowd peered into the hut in turn until all of them had seen the dangling body of Tekayo – the man they were preparing to stone. No one spoke. Such a man they knew, would have to be buried outside the village. They knew too that no newborn child would ever be named after him.

Karantina

Embakasi Airport was packed almost to capacity, and the air grew tense as the departure time approached.

Groups broke up into couples to put in a last word about the children, and one woman suddenly remembered the key to the drinks cupboard was still in her handbag.

"My goodness! Amos, the drinks key!" Dora pulled it out of her handbag and pressed it into her husband's hand.

"What is the key doing in your handbag? I thought we agreed that it should be kept on the mantelpiece."

"I am sorry darling, I was in a hurry."

"What else have you taken by mistake?" He fumbled in his pocket for the car key – it was there.

"Tafadhali sikilizeni, tafadhali sikilizeni, East African Airways inatangaza kuondoka kwa ndege yao EC 722 kwenda Entebbe, Cairo na London. Wasafiri wote wanaulizwa kuelekea kwenye ndege, Ahsante."

The passengers moved towards the departure gate. Dora clung to Amos and squeezed him close.

"Look after yourself – and please call the doctor if the children are ill."

They hugged close again and then let go as the flight call boomed out a second time in English.

At the gangway, the passengers hesitated and waved to numerous hands on the roof of the airport building. Dora thought she saw Amos.

She entered the plane and took her seat in the rear part near the window.

They fastened their seat belts on the orders of a sweet, feminine voice that welcomed them aboard the plane on behalf of Captain Wallace.

Angelina and Alice, sitting next to Dora, fixed their eyes on the little windows in the hope of catching a last glimpse of their loved ones.

Beside Dora, Milka sat tight on her seat; she had never been inside a plane before, and it looked longer and wider than she had expected.

The uneasiness made her forget her husband temporarily and she eased her tight seatbelt nervously, almost regretting that she had agreed to travel by plane.

Her heart was thudding aloud. But the take-off was smooth, and she soon fell asleep – not stirring until several hours later when the air hostess was announcing that they were about to land at Cairo Airport.

The women were all looking forward to the brief stop at Cairo – the gate of the Orient, half African half Arab where they were to change planes.

Many friends had strongly recommended a visit to the oriental bazaar in Cairo. It has almost become a place of pilgrimage for tourists from all over the world, and is famous for dangling earrings, leather bags on which the head of a beautiful oriental queen is embossed, and delicate ivory products.

They wrapped themselves up and moved shoulder to shoulder towards two airport buses that stood by. Dora looked at her watch: it was 4.30 am. Cairo was very chilly at this time.

They entered a bus that took them to an unheated airport waiting-room. The wind was bitingly cold around their ankles.

At the health desk, a plump man with a big flat head, big eyes and bushy eyebrows examined their documents without raising his head. When satisfied he waved the passengers through the narrow iron gate to the visa and passport desk – again without looking at them. On each side of him stood two smallish men in brown overalls.

Dora handed her documents to an officer and waited. There was something she resented about the whole attitude of these men who showed no interest in the travellers. She was anxious to finish as quickly as possible, and as she looked around her, enthusiasm for Cairo began to subside.

"Not good." The man threw one certificate in Dora's direction, keeping the other.

"You not go through, you diseased," he said in pidgin English.

And while Dora was looking round for someone who knew the health regulations to explain to her what was wrong, one of the men in brown overalls sprang up and dragged her by the arm, away from the queue.

The other passengers looked puzzled. Angelina, Alice and Milka who were already at the passport desk rushed back to the scene. But the other man in brown overalls barred their way with the words: "You pass through here only once. You not going back." "You pass through here only once. You not going back."

"But our friend is detained out there, we must go back and see what is wrong." Angelina was almost in tears.

"No," the man waved them back to the passport desk. "Visa pleez," the man at the desk demanded. The women looked at one another.

"They told us we don't need visas to go to Germany," Angelina butted in, brushing Alice aside.

"They go Germany ha, ha, ha ..., the man shouted to the others sitting next to him. They all laughed and then stopped suddenly like automata.

"Visa pleez – you need visa. If not, you back in the plane. You don't go in Cairo."

"We can't go back into the plane." Alice's voice was hoarse with fury. "Our plane does not leave until tomorrow at 3.30am in the morning."

"In that case buy visa."

"The German Embassy told us we don't need visas – and moreover we have no money," she said apprehensively.

"Too bad." The man threw his hands in the air. And, judging by the torrent of Arabic words that came out of his mouth, it was obvious he did not mean well.

"How much is the visa?" Angelina asked, realising the hopelessness of further argument.

"Thirty piastres," the man answered carelessly.

"I suppose we have to pay," Angelina turned to the others. "We are keeping all these people waiting."

"But how much is 30 piastres?" Alice grumbled. "Ask him!"

But instead of asking, Angelina pulled out a five pound note from her handbag and gave it to the man.

"Let him take what he wants, and you can refund it to me later."

"What is this?" the man asked aggressively.

"Money," Angelina said with sullen defiance.

"Not this." The man threw the note back to her. "I want Egyptian money, your money no value."

"But what do we do? We have no Egyptian money." Tears started in Angelina's eyes.

"Go to bank."

"Go to the bank ... where? Honestly these people!"

One of the men in brown overalls came forward and beckoned at Angelina.

"Only one with money come."

Angelina followed the man blindly. They passed through several passages till they arrived at a *bureau de change.*

A grey-haired man peered at her through the glass window. She took out the five pound note and tossed it in front of him.

The cashier took the money without looking up. He opened a drawer before him and pulled out numerous small notes. Then he counted before Angelina 500 piastres.

There was not a trace of life on his face; it looked as though he hated what he was doing.

Angelina took the money and held it tight in her hand. She walked faster to catch up with the man who had brought her to the bank and who was almost running now.

The queue had thinned down at the passport desk, with her friends leaning on iron rails, waiting impatiently.

Angelina joined the queue and waited. She looked away from the others to conceal the tears which were dribbling down her cheeks. Presently she was before the visa man. She took the whole lot of notes and threw them on the desk before the man. "You take what you want."

"You rich girl," the man mocked her.

Angelina refused to smile. The man took three notes and gave her four forms and some change back.

"Thank you," she said without looking at him, and put the rest of the money in her purse.

They were approaching the exit gate when they remembered that Dora had been detained at the health desk.

"Alice, you try and go back," Angelina suggested.

"The man has prevented us from going back once, and if we try again now he will simply flare up."

"All right, take my hand luggage – I shall try my luck. Go and find somewhere to sit."

Alice thought of what to do. She was certain the man at the passport desk would not let her go through again, and even if she did get through, the man at the health desk was very hostile.

What could she do? Immediately a thought came to her. She started to sob loudly, and because of accumulated emotional and physical strain, tears ran down her cheeks, wetting her leather coat.

"What's the matter, woman?" One of the men in brown overalls asked her, barring her way.

"Him, him," Alice pointed at the man sitting at the health desk.

Seeing that she was very wild, the man let her through the gate, and when Alice reached the passport desk, she was sobbing even louder.

The two men there looked at one another puzzled.

"What is it, madam, you sick?"

"No, I am not sick." Alice covered her face. "I want my sister – I cannot leave my sister behind!'

The men talked for a few minutes in Arabic. It was a conspiratorial whisper. Then turning to Alice, one of them said, "Your sister has not valid certificate – yellow fever. Your sister is not to go in Cairo. Sorry madam."

"But we cannot leave her in this cold airport alone," Alice burst into tears again.

"No, she does not stay here. She go to Karantina – very good place, very good. Sisters good – good like hotel."

"No, she must come with us."

"Then you see doctor."

Alice was escorted by the man in overalls to the health desk. The man in charge still sat there; and with his hands folded on the desk he resembled an Egyptian Sphinx.

Alice looked at his iron face. He could not be more than 45 years old, and yet his furrowed face made him look well over 70 years. Before Alice could open her mouth, he spoke.

"Your sister diseased. Yellow fever – she does not go in Cairo, she stay in Karantina!'

"What is this Karantina?" Alice threw her hands in the air.

"Quarantine," someone standing nearby told her. She was not familiar with medical terms, let alone their Egyptian versions.

"Where is that? I must stay with her."

"No, you cannot stay with her. She stays with other diseased persons. You are well, you go Cairo."

Alice became even more hysterical. She wept and shouted. For the first time the man revealed that he had feelings. He held her shoulders and said, "Look madam – all right. We do this."

Alice, stopped crying and looked at him.

"We do this, madam. Your sister go in Karantina now, and at nine in the morning the big doctor come. Your sister ask the big doctor to go out. The big doctor very good and kind. He let your sister to go Cairo!'

"Why don't you let her go with us now? Please, please. I beg of you."

"No, madam. I only small doctor, I don't give diseased permission to go in Cairo."

All Alice's tactics had failed. She was somewhat crestfallen at the way her histrionic gambit had misfired. She only wanted permission now to see Dora to explain to her that there was at least this last hope of the big doctor.

"Can I say goodbye to my sister then?"

"All right, she is there."

Alice found Dora shivering in a little cubicle. She was not crying, but was clutching her handbag with both hands and staring into space.

Alice burst into tears again, but Dora got up and laughed.

"Goodness, Alice, don't take it too seriously. I suppose I will be all right ... if only they would stop calling me a diseased person."

At that point Alice too laughed amid her tears.

"I hope they are not taking you to a mortuary, the way they insist that you are diseased frightens me." Alice hugged her. "All right dearest I shall speak to our Ambassador and ask him to get in touch with you. And we shall definitely come back to see you as soon as we are settled in our hotel."

Alice pressed Dora's hands affectionately and then left. A pang of pain flashed through Dora's heart but she managed to cheek her tears.

"Ambulance here, madam, we go."

Dora obeyed. She followed the man in brown overalls who had been waiting to take her away. The place was cold, but her body was warm with perspiration. Her fingers trembled like those of an alcoholic.

They reached a big door and the man flung it wide open. Dora could not see an ambulance, but there was a dingy, grey van which had no windows standing nearby.

"Where is the ambulance?"

"There, madam." The man pointed at the grey van.

"That is no ambulance," Dora protested. "That is a Black Maria."

The man threw his hands in the air.

"You go in, that is ambulance,"

The driver sat on his seat puffing some kind of cigar. Its fumes were bitter and they hit Dora forcibly as she entered the van.

The driver did not move, nor did he turn his head to look at his passenger.

To her great surprise, Dora found three other passengers sitting inside. Perhaps they were also "diseased".

It was dark inside, and she could not, therefore, tell who her new companions were.

A man made room for her. Then a porter entered the van and sat next to the driver. He banged the door and they left the airport for Karantina. No one spoke.

The van stopped abruptly about a mile from the airport. The driver hooted three times and a big iron gate opened. He drove inside the high thick walls which reminded Dora of Fort Jesus at Mombasa, and up to an oblong stone building.

Dawn was just breaking and the wind was very cold. The passengers jumped down from the van, and it was then that Dora discovered that one of the passengers was an African.

"Hello," the man greeted her.

"Hello," replied Dora shyly.

She was not in the mood to talk. Why couldn't the man leave her alone!

The other two passengers were European, and the woman was wiping her eyes – perhaps she was crying.

A thick wooden door opened and they were ushered into a large lounge. The driver who had kept quiet throughout now wanted money.

"I have no Egyptian money," Dora pleaded with him. "I thought this was an ambulance!"

"Yes, this ambulance – but I wan't money for smoke." He pointed his cigar towards Dora.

"I will pay him." The man whom Dora did not want to talk to came to her rescue. "How much?" the man asked the driver.

"Give what you have to give me," the driver said in a low voice.

"Give us both," the porter interjected.

The African brought out an Egyptian note from his jacket pocket and thrust it into the driver's hand. "For you and the porter."

"Sank you, Sir."

Then they left Dora and the other passengers standing in the lounge with their luggage.

On the sofas in the lounge a group of nurses were just getting up from sleep.

Dora looked at her watch: it was 6.15 am – their ordeal had lasted two hours. Her legs were aching and her toes were sore inside the light shoes she wore.

The nurses bundled their blankets together onto one sofa and then came to them barefooted, with their smooked uniforms badly creased.

They took the luggage without uttering a word and carried it towards a corridor that led to individual rooms.

Dora and the other passengers followed on. The nurses entered a small room which looked like an office.

An obese lady in a black dress lifted her head from the table on which she had been having a little snooze. She had a long face, and her dark hair which lacked any lustre was done in large circular curls which made her head look smaller than it really was.

She still looked sleepy and there was a dark line under her lower eyelids. She bubbled some words to the passengers in Arabic. "We don't know Arabic," they told her.

"I, no English," she threw her hands in the air. She waved her hands at one of the nurses who went running out. Presently a porter came in.

After a brief *tete-a-tete,* he said, "The sister is saying you want breakfast or no?"

The European couple said, "Yes." The African man said he wanted breakfast, but not at the time. Dora, still puzzled after hearing that the woman was a medical Sister, stood speechless. "You also want?" the porter put the question to Dora directly. "Yes, later."

The Sister said something and the porter translated. "Sister say, you want breakfast pay now." "How can we pay for what we haven't even seen?" the African gentleman retorted, and he asked the porter to protest to the Sister. "sister say breakfast 44 piastres you want to eat it at eight or nine o'clock you pay now and get receipt."

The European couple said if that was the case then they did not want breakfast. The porter then gave this warning from the Sister: "Sister say, it is up to you. Lunch a long way. We don't give lunch till 3.00 pm"

He grabbed the hand of the man and pointed at three o'clock on his watch.

"What do you think darling?"

The lady who was either his wife or his fiancée replied, "All right, lets have it."

"Two breakfasts," the man said, pulling out an Egyptian note with the figure "100" on. He placed it on the table before the Sister. She wrote them a receipt and gave them back the change.

"Blast them," the European man cursed, as one of the nurses led them to their room.

Dora suddenly realised that she had only one East African pound note. She pulled it out of her purse and gave it to the Sister.

"No value." She threw the money aside.

"But I have no Egyptian money," Dora pleaded. "Would you like travellers' cheques?"

"No, no, no, Egyptian money."

"Don't worry, I will pay for her." The African gentleman handed over an Egyptian note of 100 piastres to the sister who gave him two receipts. A girl then took Dora and her rescuer to their rooms.

In the corridor the porter who had been translating demanded money from them.

"Goodness – these people are getting on my nerves," the man complained. "Look," he told the porter, "go and ask those Europeans for money. I had paid the ambulance driver!"

But he would not let him free.

"My God ..." he smacked his lips peevishly, and then in disgust, threw some coins at the porter-interpreter.

At 6.30 am the sun was visible and small rays of light were now illuminating the paved yard of this fortress. All doors were still closed – perhaps the inmates were still asleep.

In the yard stood several iron beds which must have been left out for disinfection.

Dora's heart leapt with fear. Were there infectious diseases here? Had people died on those beds? She had only seen beds taken out for disinfection and airing whenever someone died at their hospital.

She counted eight beds in all, and a cold chill was still running along her spine when she reached her room.

A large "V" was painted in red on the door. The paint looked very much like dry blood. The girl who had brought her suitcase to the room had disappeared.

There was not a single window open and the smell of dust hit Dora's nose as she entered the room. She struggled with the window facing the corridor and pulled it open inwards. Then she pushed up the wooden blind that kept out the light.

One look at the room was enough to drive her out of it. Dust had accumulated in all the four corners; cobwebs were everywhere; the sheets had obviously been slept in and there was a black mark on the pillow which must have been left by someone's greasy hair. Dora bumped into the porter as she walked back to the Sister's office.

"What you want, madam?" the porter asked.

"I want to tell the sister that my room is filthy and I cannot sleep in it," she said wearily, without hope of a reasonable answer.

"You cannot see sister, madam. Sister asleep. Come, I will take you to a clean room."

Dora followed the porter to another room six doors from room "V". The windows were at least open there and the smell of dust was not so powerful.

"You be here, madam. At eight o'clock the girl come and sweep the room."

Dora was still talking to the porter when the African gentleman joined them.

"By the way, my name is Banale – I come from Zambia."

"Mine is Dora Owiti – Mrs of course. I come from Kenya."

"Why don't we sit in the lounge, the rooms are so dirty and the porter tells me that they will be swept at eight. I honestly don't want to be sick – I have a very heavy programme ahead of me."

"Well, that seems to be the most sensible thing to do," Dora said rather reluctantly.

"The lounge may not be clean, but at least it is large and the air can circulate."

The nurses had woken up in the lounge and two of them were wiping the floor with a wet cloth. Dora sank into a chair and fell asleep almost immediately.

At 8.30 am her sleep was interrupted – it was breakfast time, Mr Banale led the way.

The breakfast consisted of rolls, some white fat that looked like margarine but tasted quite different, a small jug of camel's milk and a small cold omelette in the centre of a big white plate.

A large fly that had been enjoying the rolls on Dora's plate flew off and perched upon a curtain nearby.

"This is really a conspiracy," she said. "Why do they insist on dishing the food out half an hour before they call us to eat it? Can't we dish it out ourselves?"

Dora put the omelette plate aside. In her mind, she could see numerous fly eggs on it, which made her tummy queasy. She removed the outer layers of the rolls and ate what was left.

When breakfast was over, they returned to the lounge to wait for the big doctor whom they had been assured would release them. Inside the quarantine 'hospital' it was quite light now. The desert sunlight was shining brightly in the yard. All the windows of the lounge were barred, and heavy curtains remained undrawn. The door leading to the main compound was also locked.

"Oh come on, don't be so thoughtful," Mr Banale coaxed Dora. "You can always turn lemon into lemonade! The doctor is coming at 9.30 am. We may be lucky to get out of this terrible place. We could then ring our embassies to come for us at the gate. Your First Secretary here is a friend of Mr Tika, our Ambassador, and there shouldn't be any difficulty in getting transport."

"Thank you. I would really love to get out of this dungeon. The whole thing is ridiculous. The doctor in Nairobi told me that if I have my old yellow fever certificate, a re–vaccination certificate is valid immediately."

"These health regulations are international. Oh, I am thoroughly disgusted."

Resentment stirred in her and overflowed in an almost incoherent torrent of words.

Dora looked at her watch – it was 8.55 am and the doctor was not due until half past nine. They sat in silence and the European couple joined them.

They sat with their backs to Dora and Banale, the woman resting her head on the man's shoulder. She seemed to be crying.

The man turned to her and rubbed his lips on her cheeks; but she did not seem impressed. Then he got out a handkerchief and dabbed it on her eyes. He whispered something into her ears and coaxed her for some time like a nannie coaxing a hungry baby.

"I bet those two were on their way to a honeymoon! What a start!" Dora laughed. "She is probably weeping her eyes out because she thinks this may be a bad omen. You know how superstitious Europeans are about weddings and honeymoons.

Things must go well with the honeymoon even if the marriage fails later."

"Honeymoons are a waste of money," Banale affirmed. "You have a visitor for whom the whole family had been waiting – and instead of spending the first three or four days of marriage rejoicing with home people, you run away with her to an expensive hotel to spend some miserable time together. How selfish! We must keep some of our good traditions."

"Are you married?" Dora interrupted.

"Of course I am and we have one child."

"What kind of honeymoon did you have?"

"Me! I am not a European. I had a proper wedding."

"What do you mean by a proper wedding?" Dora asked him laughing.

"Well, we were married at the Cathedral in Lusaka, my bride was accompanied by twelve bridesmaids."

"That must have been a big wedding," Dora interjected.

"Yes, a big one. After the ceremony, we gave a reception for about 500 guests in the Cathedral hall – in European fashion. Then my bride, the bridesmaids, my relatives and myself drove to my home about 30 miles from Lusaka to have a proper African wedding.

"We were met by singing and dancing relatives, all of whom were carrying green leaves. Anna – my wife, alighted from our car and as she was being unveiled before my grandmother, a big cry from the women filled the air.

"My grandmother nodded her approval, and they rubbed a coin on her forehead. Then we were both led to the arena that had been built for the occasion.

"I had never seen Anna looking so beautiful and composed! She sat on a platform and proudly watched the women dancing, while the men showered many gifts on her. Eating and drinking took two complete days and on the third day we went back to the city to start life on our own."

"It must have been a marvellous wedding," Dora said, visibly impressed. "I can just imagine how proud you must have been, especially when your grandmother expressed her satisfaction with your choice."

"Yes, those days are still so fresh in my mind."

"Didn't Anna ask for a honeymoon?"

"To tell you the truth, that was quite a problem. You see, Anna was a town girl, and she had read all these European stories about wonderful honeymoons – I made it clear to her that I wanted a proper African wedding with my people. On the other hand and I am now speaking to you as fellow African – I told her to be frank with me: if she was not a virgin then I was prepared to run away with her soon after the reception at the Cathedral."

"Nonsense," Dora laughed at the top of her voice, and for a moment the sorrow she was feeling about her misfortune vanished. "You are being rude," she told him.

"I am not being rude. Even with the Europeans – and I have studied their culture, there was a time when a woman's virginity was regarded as a very important quality. Not to be a virgin at marriage was a social stigma that was difficult to live down.

"That is still the case in many African societies. But when the European girls took to eating the forbidden fruit in a big way, they could not stay home to face their inquisitive relatives. So the idea of a honeymoon was born. Today it is regarded as one of the hallmarks of a civilised wedding."

Dora laughed. She was almost convinced by Banale's theory about the origin of the European honeymoon but she did not want to admit it.

"Are you sure you are not just making the story up because you didn't have a honeymoon? Sour grapes!"

"Me!" Banale laughed. "I know what is good for me. It is the women who don't know what is good for them. What is the use of locking yourself up with a man you are going to see all your life instead of being spoilt with songs and dances by your in-laws? After all you can only be a bride once."

The conversation was brought to an abrupt end when a fat lady with flaccid breasts wearing a white uniform walked into the lounge.

She first talked to the European couple, and then moved to Dora and Banale. Unlike the night Sister, she had a ready smile that illuminated her beautiful face.

"Did you have any breakfast?"

"Yes. Thank you, Sister," Dora replied; but Banale kept quiet. Dora looked at her watch – it was already ten o'clock.

"When is the doctor coming, Sister."

"Oh doctor! You want him?" Sister asked puzzled.

"Yes, we both want him."

"What you want him for?"

"Well, they told me at that airport that I should see him about my yellow fever certificate. The doctor at the airport said it is only the big doctor who can let me free, because my certificate is ..."

But the Sister cut Dora short.

"The doctor at the airport say you can get out of here? Never! He cheated you."

"But he told me this several times, Sister," Dora argued. "Please, let me speak to the doctor."

"Madam, you see doctor, you waste time. I sure doctor don't get you out of here till tomorrow. You sit and rest." Then she hurried away.

A very big lump blocked Dora's throat and choked her till she felt tears rolling down her cheeks. Banale looked away.

"Have you ever met such heartless people?" Dora sniffed.

The couple sitting in front of them turned round to look at her as she spoke. It was obvious they all shared her sentiments.

"Just pull yourself together and pretend you are on holiday. With only 18 hours to go, your position is much better than mine. I still have two whole nights in this place."

"And what do I do with these 18 hours?" Dora cried out wildly.

"Sit down and relax," Banale teased her.

Dora looked away from him wishing she could have half his patience.

It was 10.30. The morning was getting warmer. A number of weary-looking people entered the lounge.

"I wonder where that one is going?"

Banale drew Dora's attention to a very old man who took a seat at the far end of the room. He could have been 65 years old and he was perhaps the darkest man Dora had ever seen, although his hair was absolutely white.

He looked hungry and sad.

"Let us go and talk to him." Banale stood up. Dora followed him to the big sofa where the old man was sitting.

"Good morning," they greeted him almost simultaneously.

"Good morning," he answered with a broad smile.

"We hope we are not interfering. Where do you come from? And where are you going?"

The old man threw his hands in the air —

"No English – Portuguese?" They shook their heads sadly. "– French?"

"No French," Banale replied.

"And madame?"

"No French," Dora told him.

The old man got up without warning and disappeared towards the rooms. Presently he returned with a young man who looked like a student.

"Good morning. The old man tells me that you want to speak to him. I speak a little French and so I can translate for you."

"Yes, please," Dora said. "We asked him where he comes from and where he is going."

"That I can tell you madame," the young man said, "because we have now been here for three days. He is a political refugee from Angola. He has come here to trace some members of his party who fled from Angola about a year ago; and he has suffered here terribly. When we arrived two days ago, he misplaced his yellow fever certificate. The doctor at the airport refused to accept his explanation. So they vaccinated him and he is to stay in quarantine for ten days."

"How terrible!" Banale said.

The elderly man pulled out a huge wallet, and after uttering a stream of words in French he produced some money and put it on the table.

"What is he saying?" Dora asked the young interpreter.

"He is saying that he is likely to die here of hunger, because he has these Ghana notes, which the people here say have no value. Yesterday, he ordered breakfast and sent the money to the airport to be changed, and they sent it back saying it was valueless. He then asked the Sister if he could be allowed to go to town to change it. She just said 'never' and walked away. He has pleaded with them in vain for two days. I give him a bit of my food, but that is insufficient."

"Poor dear!" Dora's tears collected.

"They imprison him here and then refuse to accept his money. How do they expect him to get food? The whole world is paying lip service to brotherhood of mankind – that is what it is. These people are no brothers to anyone."

The old man looked appealingly at Banale as though he had power to change Ghana money into piastres.

"Tell the old man that we will take up his case with the doctor. They must either change the money for him or allow him to go and change it in town or else give him free food."

The young man translated Banale's words to the refugee. A hopeful smile came to his face. He put his hands together as if praying to God and murmured something. Then he heaved a deep sigh and let his hands fall limply on his lap.

The morning wore on slowly. Dora was still nursing the hope of seeing the doctor but there was no sign of any man in a white overall.

Eventually she fell asleep on the sofa. When Banale tapped at her hands, it was 1.30 pm.

"My goodness, have you all had lunch?"

"Didn't they tell us that lunch will be served between 3.00 and 4.00 pm.? There is still plenty of time."

"Then why did you wake me up?" Dora yawned.

"Well, you are the only person left here. I thought you may not be safe. Why don't you go and sleep in your room. It has been swept." Suddenly Dora became afraid and jumped to her feet.

"All right, wake me up when lunch is ready." She walked to her room. It was a little cleaner now, but the sheets still looked slept in. She removed her national costume which was about three yards long, spread it on the bed and then lay on it. She did not fall asleep. She lay there thinking of her friends till Banale banged at her door at 3.15 pm.

There were several people sitting at the table. The lunch, which consisted of salad, thin slices of meat and boiled potatoes, was stone cold. A big yellow orange and a bun were on a side plate. Everybody ate in silence. Dora only ate the bun and orange, leaving the rest of her food to the Angola refugee. He was grateful for it. At the end of the meal most of the food remained piled up high in the plates. As people were leaving the lounge a porter shouted, "You want supper at night?" Nobody answered.

"If you want supper at night pay now. Supper comes at ten o'clock. Only 99 piastres, pay now. I give you receipt or else no supper."

There was no choice. They bought their supper tickets at 4.00 pm. Mr Banale, Dora, and a few other passengers spent the rest of the evening watching Arabic films on television.

Dinner was brought in at nine, which was an hour earlier than the time originally announced by the porter. Dora again shared her food with the old man. When he was told that she would be catching her plane to Germany at three in the morning he wept, but Dora assured him that God would find another way for him.

"Who is Dora?" A barefooted nurse interrupted their conversation.

"Yes?" Dora looked up nervously.

"Madam telafon." Dora jumped to her feet and followed the nurse.

"There, speak."

She lifted the receiver, her hands trembling. "Hello, hello."

There was a pause and then a faint voice answered. "Hello, Dora are you still there?"

"Just," – she was almost in tears. "This place is terrible, worse than a prison. Just pray for me that I come out of here alive!'

"Oh Dora," Alice blew her nose, "We have been trying the whole day to see you, but they would not let us. They even refused to give us the telephone number of the place.

"How are you all?" Dora cut Alice short. To dwell on her misfortune would only make her cry. It was better to hear about their impression of Cairo and their shopping expeditions which she had missed.

"You won't believe our story," Alice lamented. "You should have seen us. We got into a taxi at the airport and gave the driver the name of the hotel we were booked in. He showed complete surprise and said there must be a mistake. But we insisted we were right. After a short argument, he threw his hands in the air and said: "I take you."

"Oh, Dora, we were shocked. We found that we had been booked in a warehouse – a very dirty shanty in a back street on the outskirts of the city.

"The hotel man was even more surprised to see us. He gave us an ominous look, and said they were full up. So we went back to the airport cursing everybody.

"In fact Angelina wanted to return home by tonight's plane. The taxi driver kept repeating, obviously with some relish, 'I told you'."

"And where are you now?" Dora gasped.

"Well, we decided to be tough and demanded a good hotel. After a long argument we were finally brought here at 2.30 pm only to find that lunch time was up. I am quite sick and seriously I am thinking of returning home. I think Angelina was right."

They paused for a few seconds.

"Shocking my dear! I see there is much to talk about when we meet at the airport. You never know who is listening in these telephones. We'd better not say any more."

"Get some sleep," Alice advised.

"You do the same and greet the others." The telephone clicked when the receiver was replaced the other side, but Dora hung on for a while listening.

The start of their journey had been full of misfortunes. She wondered what awaited them at their destination.

Dora told Banale what had happened to her friends and they both swore never to follow the Cairo route again. At 10.00 pm. Dora retired to her room. The night sister told her, "I wake you at two o'clock, ambulance take you to airport."

She washed and changed into her travelling clothes. She had said goodbye to the nurses and to her friends, including the old refugee.

She prayed for her husband and children and then stretched herself out on the bed as she had done in the afternoon. The night was cool and Dora slept well. At two o'clock sharp they woke her up.

"Ambulance is here, ambulance is here."

Dora jumped up, put on her coat and locked her suitcase. She was in such a hurry to leave that she even forgot to check in the mirror to see whether her face was clean.

The porter took her suitcase and she hurried after him along the corridor. The nurses were fast asleep on the lounge sofas. The door opened and for the first time in 20 hours Dora, stepped out into the outer yard.

The morning was very chilly. She entered at the back of the ambulance and the door was shut.

The iron gate opened and the ambulance moved out into the free world.

Dora managed to catch a last glimpse of "Karantina" through the driver's window as the ambulance sped away towards the airport.

The Green Leaves

It was a dream. Then the sounds grew louder. Nyagar threw the blanket off his ears and listened. Yes, he was right. Heavy footsteps and voices were approaching. He turned round to wake up his wife. She was not there. He got up and rushed to the door. It was unlocked. Where was Nyamundhe? "How could she slip back to her hut so quietly?" he wondered. "I've told her time and again never to leave my hut without waking me up to bolt the door. She will see me tomorrow!"

"*Ero, ero,* there, there!" The noise was quite close now – about thirty yards away. Nyagar put a sheet round his well-developed body, fumbled for his spear and club and then left the hut.

"*Piti, piti. Piti, piti.*" A group was running towards his gate. He opened the gate and hid by the fence. Nyagar did not want to meet the group directly, as he was certain some dangerous person was being pursued.

Three or four men ran past the gate, and then a larger group followed. He emerged from his hiding place and followed them.

"These bastards took all my six bulls," he heard one voice cursing.

"Don't worry they will pay for it," another voice replied.

Nyagar had caught up with the pursuing crowd. He now realised that the three or four men he had seen run past his gate were cattle thieves. They rounded a bend. About thirty yards away were three figures who could only be the thieves.

"They must not escape," a man shouted.

"They will not," the crowd answered in chorus.

The gap was narrowing. The young moon had disappeared, and it was quite dark.

"Don't throw a spear," an elder warned. "If it misses, they can use it against us."

The thieves took the wrong turning. They missed the bridge across the River Opok, which separated the people of Masala from those of Mirogi. Instead they turned right. While attempting to cross the river, they suddenly found themselves in a whirlpool. Hastily they scrambled out of the water.

"Ero, ero," a cry went out from the pursuers. Before the thieves could find a safe place at which to cross the river, the crowd was upon them. With their clubs they smote the thieves to the ground. The air was filled with the howls of the captured men. But the crowd showed no mercy.

During the scuffle, one of the thieves escaped and disappeared into the thick bush by the river.

"Follow him! Follow him!" someone shouted. Three men ran in the direction in which he had disappeared, breathing heavily. The bush was thick and thorny. They stood still and listened. There was no sound. They beat the bush around with their clubs – still no sound. He had escaped.

Another thief took out his knife and drove it into the shoulder-blade of one of the pursuers, who fell back with the knife still sticking in him. In the ensuing confusion, the thief got up and made straight for the whirlpool. To everybody's amazement, he was seen swimming effortlessly across it to the other side of the river.

Nyagar plucked the knife from Omoro's shoulder and put his hand over the wound to stop the bleeding. Omoro, still shaken, staggered to his feet and leaned on Nyagar. Streaks of blood were still running along his back, making his buttocks wet.

One thief was lying on the grass, groaning. As the other two had escaped, the crowd were determined to make an example of this one. They hit him several times on the head and chest. He groaned and stretched out his arms and legs as if giving up the ghost.

"Aa, aa," Omoro raised his voice. "Let not the enemy die in your hands. His spirit would rest upon our village. Let him give up the ghost when we have returned to our huts."

The crowd heeded Omoro's warning. They tore green leaves from nearby trees and covered the victim completely with them. They would call the entire clan in the morning to come and bury him by the riverside.

The men walked back home in silence, Omoro's shoulder had stopped bleeding. He walked, supported by two friends who volunteered to take him home. It was still not light, but their eyes were by now accustomed to the darkness. They reached Nyagar's home – the gate was still ajar.

"Remember to be early tomorrow," a voice told him. 'We must be on the scene to stop the women before they start going to the river."

Nyagar entered his home, while the others walked on without looking back. The village was hushed. The women must have been awake, but they dared not talk to their husbands. Whatever had happened, they thought, they would hear about it in the morning. Having satisfied themselves that their husbands were safely back, they turned over and slept.

Nyagar entered his hut, searched for his medicine bag and found it in a corner. He opened it, and pulled out a bamboo container. He uncorked the container, and then scooped out some ash from it. He placed a little on his tongue, mixed it well with saliva and then swallowed. He put some on his palm and blew it in the direction of the gate. As he replaced the bamboo container in the bag, his heart felt at peace.

He sat on the edge of his bed. He started to remove his clothes. Then he changed his mind. Instead he just sat there, staring vacantly into space. Finally he made up his mind to go back to the dead man alone.

He opened the door slowly, and then closed it quietly after him. No one must hear him.

He did not hesitate at the gate, but walked blindly on.

"Did I close the gate?" he wondered. He looked back. Yes, he had closed it, or it looked close.

"He must have a lot of money in his pocket," Nyagar thought aloud.

Apart from a sinister sound which occasionally rolled through the night, everything was silent. Dawn must have been approaching. The faint and golden gleams of light which usually herald the birth of a new day could be seen in the east shooting skywards from the bowels of the earth. He knew that stock thieves sold stolen cattle at the earliest opportunity.

"The others were foolish not to have searched him." He stopped and listened. Was somebody coming? No. He was merely hearing the echo of his own footsteps.

"Perhaps the other two thieves who had escaped are now back at the scene," he thought nervously. "No, they can't be there – they wouldn't be such idiots as to hang around there."

The heap of green leaves came in sight. A numb paralysing pain ran through his spine. He thought his heart had stopped beating. He stopped to check. It was still beating, all right. He was just nervous. He moved on faster, and the echo of his footsteps bothered him.

When Nyagar reached the scene of murder, he noticed that everything was exactly as they had left it earlier. He stood there for a while, undecided. He looked in all directions to ensure that no one was coming. There was nobody. He was all alone with the dead body. He now felt nervous. "Why should you disturb a dead body?" His inner voice asked him." 'What do you want to do with money? You have three wives and twelve children. You have many cattle and enough food. What more do you want?" The voice persisted. He felt even more nervous, and was about to retreat when an urge stronger than his will egged him on.

"You have come all this far for one cause only, and the man is lying before you. You only need to put your hand in his pockets, and all the money will be yours. Don't deceive yourself that you have enough wealth. Nobody in the world has enough wealth."

Nyagar bent over the dead man, and hurriedly removed the leaves from him. His hand came in contact with the man's arm which lay folded on his chest. It was still warm. A chill ran through him again, and he stood up. It was unusual for a dead person to be warm, he thought. However, he dismissed the thought. Perhaps he was just nervous and was imagining things. He bent over the man again, and rolled him on his back. He looked dead all right.

He fumbled quickly to find the pockets. He dipped his hand into the first pocket. It was empty. He searched the second pocket – that, too, was empty. A pang of disappointment ran through his heart. Then he remembered that cattle traders often carried their money in a small bag stringed with a cord round their neck.

He knelt beside the dead man and found his neck. Sure enough there was a string tied around his neck, from which hung a little bag. A triumphant smile played at the corners of his mouth. Since he had no knife with which to cut the string, he decided to remove it over the man's head. As Nyagar lifted the man's head, there was a crashing blow on his right eye. He staggered for a few yards and fell unconscious to the ground.

The thief had just regained consciousness and was still very weak. But there was no time to lose. He managed to get up on his feet after a second attempt. His body was soaked in blood, but his mind was now clear. He gathered all the green leaves and heaped them on Nyagar. He then made for the bridge which he had failed to locate during the battle.

He walked away quickly – the spirit should not leave the body while he was still on the scene. It was nearly dawn. He would reach the river Migua in time to rinse the blood off his clothes.

Before sunrise, the clan leader Olielo sounded the funeral drum to alert the people. Within an hour more than a hundred clansmen had assembled at the foot of the Opok tree where the elders normally met to hear criminal and civil cases. Olielo then addressed the gathering.

"Listen, my people. Some of you must have heard of the trouble we had in our clan last night. Thieves broke into Omogo's kraal and stole six of his ploughing oxen."

"Oh!" the crowd exclaimed.

Olielo continued, "As a result, blood was shed, and we now have a body lying here."

"Is this so?" one elder asked.

"Yes, it is so," Olielo replied. "Now, listen to me. Although our laws prohibit any wanton killing, thieves and adulterers we regard as animals. If anyone kills one of them he is not guilty of murder. He is looked upon as a person who has rid society of an evil spirit, and in return society has a duty to protect him and his children. You all know that such a person must be cleansed before he again associates with other members of society. But the white man's laws are different. According to his laws, if you kill a man because you find him stealing your cattle or sleeping in your wife's hut, you are guilty of murder – and therefore you must also be killed. Because he thinks his laws are superior to ours, we should handle him carefully. We have ancestors – the white man has none. That is why they bury their dead far away from their houses.

"This is what we should do. We shall send thirty men to the white man to tell him that we have killed a thief. This group should tell him that the whole clan killed the thief. Take my word, my children. The white man's tricks work only among a divided people. If we stand united, none of us will be killed."

"The old man has spoken well," they shouted. Thirty men were elected, and they immediately left for the white man's camp.

More people, including some women, had arrived to swell the number of the group. They moved towards the river where the dead thief lay covered in leaves, to await the arrival of the white man.

Nyamundhe moved near her co-wife. "Where is Nyagar? My eye has not caught him."

Her co-wife peered through the crowd, and then answered, "I think he has gone with the thirty. He left home quite early. I woke up very early this morning, but the gate was open. He had left the village!"

Nyamundhe recollected that as they entered the narrow path which led to the river, their feet felt wet from the morning dew. And bending across the path as if saying prayers to welcome the dawn, were long grasses which were completely overpowered by the thick dew. She wanted to ask her co-wife where their husband could have gone but, noticing her indifference, she had decided to keep quiet.

"I did not like that black cat which dashed in front of us when we were coming here," Nyamundhe said to her co-wife.

"Yes, it is a bad sign for a black cat to cross one's way first thing in the morning."

They heard the sound of a lorry. They looked up and saw a cloud of dust and two police lorries approaching.

The two lorries pulled up by the heap of green leaves, A European police officer and four African officers stepped down. They opened the back of one of the lorries and the thirty men who had been sent to the police station by the clan came out. "Where is the clan elder?" the white officer demanded. Olielo stepped forward.

"Tell me the truth. What happened? I don't believe a word of what these people are saying. What did you send them to tell me?"

Olielo spoke sombrely and slowly in Dholuo, pronouncing every word distinctly. His words were translated by an African police officer.

"I sent them to inform you that we killed a thief last night."

"What! You killed a man?" the white man moved towards Olielo. The other policemen followed him.

"You killed a man?" the white officer repeated.

"No, we killed a thief." Olielo maintained his ground.

"How many times have I told you that you must abandon this savage custom of butchering one another? No one is a thief until he has been tried in a court of law and found guilty. Your people are deaf." The white man pointed at Olielo with his stick in an ominous manner.

"This time I shall show you how to obey the law. Who killed him?" the white officer asked angrily.

"All of us," answered Olielo, pointing at the crowd.

"Don't be silly. Who hit him first?"

The crowd was getting restless. The people surged forward menacingly towards the five police officers.

"We all hit the thief," they shouted.

"If you want to arrest us, you are free to do so. You'd better send for more lorries."

"Where is the dead man?" the white man asked Olielo.

"There," Olielo replied, pointing at the heap of leaves.

The police moved towards the heap. The crowd also pushed forward. They wanted to get a glimpse of him before the white man took him away.

The last time a man had been killed in the area, the police took the corpse to Kisumu where it was cut up into pieces and then stitched up again. Then they returned it to the people saying, "Here is your man, bury him." Some people claimed that bile is extracted from such bodies and given to police tracker dogs; and that is why the dogs can track a thief to his house. Many people believed such stories. They were sure that this body would be taken away again by the police.

The European officer told the other police officer to uncover the body. They hesitated for a while, and then obeyed.

Olielo looked at the body before them unbelievingly. Then he looked at his people, and at the police. Was he normal? Where was the thief? He looked at the body a second time. He was not insane. It was the body of Nyagar, his cousin, who lay dead, with a sizeable wooden stick driven through his right eye.

Nyamundhe broke loose from the crowd and ran towards the dead body. She fell on her husband's body and wept bitterly. Then turning to the crowd, she shouted, "Where is the thief you killed? Where is he?"

As the tension mounted, the crowd broke up into little groups of twos and threes. The women started to wail; and the men who had killed the thief that night looked at one another in complete disbelief. They had left Nyagar entering his village while they walked on. They could swear to it. Then Olielo, without any attempt to conceal his tear drenched face, appealed to his people with these words, "My countrymen, the evil hand has descended upon us. Let it not break up our society. Although Nyagar is dead, his spirit is still among us."

But Nyamundhe did not heed the comforts of Jaduong Olielo nor did she trust the men who swore that they had seen Nyagar enter his village after the incident with the thieves. She struggled wildly with the police who carried the corpse of her husband and placed it at the back of the lorry to be taken to Kisumu for a post mortem. A police officer comforted her with the promise that a village-wide inquiry would start at once into the death of her husband.

But Nyamundhe shook her head. "If you say you will give him back to me alive, then I will listen."

Nyamundhe tore her clothes and stripped to the waist. She walked slowly behind the mourners, weeping and chanting, her hands raised above her head.

> *My lover the son of Ochieng*
> *The son of Omolo*
> *The rains are coming down*
> *Yes, the rains are coming down*
> *The nights will be dark*
> *The nights will be cold and long*
> *Oh the son-in-law of my mother*
> *I have no heart to forgive,*

I have no heart to pardon
All these mourners cheat me now
Yes, they cheat me
But when the sun goes to his home and
Darkness falls, they desert me.
In the cold hours of the night
Each woman clings to her man
There is no one among them
There is none
There is no woman who will tend me a
Husband for the night
Ah, my lover, the son of Ochieng
The son-in-law of my mother.

The Empty Basket

Aloo hastened her steps. She felt nervous and panicky. It looked as though the earth under her feet was moving in the way that angry clouds race in the sky when it is going to rain. But now the earth was moving in the opposite direction pushing the hut further and further away. She started running. The distance was narrowing. She could see more people gathered on the yard close to the hut. She recognised Nyariwo, the wife of her brother-in-law whose hut was in the village next to theirs. Aloo's knees suddenly went weak and numb, and she could not run.

The crowd looked like mourners. They stood in groups facing the hut. Some women stood with hands above their heads. What could it be? The three children had been playing in the yard when she took her weeding hoe to weed the beans in a garden two miles away from the village. The baby, Akoth, now seven months, was in good health. Ouma, just two years old, had waved her goodbye, and Anyango the little nurse, the daughter of Aloo's uncle, who had lived with the family for two years was a good little girl who managed both children well. But Aloo knew that the crowd could not be there for nothing. Some misfortune must have befallen the three children.

Aloo crossed the little path that led to the river. The voices of the people greeted her ears but she could not make out if they were mourning or arguing. Long grass creeping on the path entangled her right foot and she nearly fell down. Then, amid the voices of adults, Aloo heard the shrill voice of a child crying. She recognised it as the voice of Anyango the little nurse. Yes, one of her children had met with fate.

Aloo threw down the hoe and a bundle of firewood she was carrying. As she entered the gate, Anyango ran toward her empty-handed, her face flooded with tears. "What has happened to the baby?" Aloo whispered. She could have asked louder but the words refused to leave her throat. When Anyango did not answer, she brushed her aside and joined the group. Then everybody was speaking to her at the same time and their voices rang out in her ears, yet she did not really catch what they were saying. Little Ouma ran and clung to her, but she did not look down or talk to him.

Then Aloo's eyes rested on a shambles of broken chairs and tables. She had left them neatly arranged in the middle of the sitting room. She turned stiffly to the crowd. A man was telling her that a huge snake had entered the house, the biggest snake they had ever seen in Kagonya. At first the snake circled in a heap near the dining room table with its head raised to the door, the man went on. "For half an hour we have been hitting the Satan, and it would not move. Then when Omolo hit its neck it crawled like a ghost and went and made a heap on top of the bed!" The man hesitated and looked at the others anxiously. "The baby is in there, Aloo. We can't get her out. That snake is ready to strike even from the bedroom door."

Aloo stood there hypnotised by the words which she could not believe were true. Then a vicious mood seized her and she lashed out at the men standing by. "All this time I thought that I was married to a clan of men – all this time! Why didn't someone tell me that there were no men in this clan. All, all of you are cowardly women." She had pushed her son away and was standing at the bedroom door. Then the vicious mood left her. Instead, a numbness that had crept from her head completely paralysed her body. She shook involuntarily. Perhaps it was the furious beating of her heart that made her body shake so.

The snake's puffy head was raised well above its curled body sunk comfortably in the middle of Aloo's bed. Not far away from the snake the baby Akoth lay peacefully asleep on a basket cot supported on two table chairs. The baby was still breathing all right. Perhaps the snake had not noticed it? Aloo felt sick in her stomach, the snake heaved a little as if aware that Aloo, was declaring open war on it. But Aloo did not move. She stood there dazed, her eyes fixed on the snake and her heart burning for the baby daughter who had brought so much happiness to her life. Then the snake turned its head slightly, its tongue waggling furiously. It looked as though it was telling Aloo, "I give you only one minute," for when it had waggled its tongue like that, it turned its head towards the wall and started descending under the bed away from the baby.

Everything was over within seconds. In the yard, Aloo sat weeping slowly, her plump baby in her arms, her body soaked in perspiration. When the baby pulled her left breast through a torn hole in her dress and struggled to push it in her mouth, she did not stop her. She could not quite remember what happened during that ghastly few seconds when she snatched the baby from the cot. All she remembered was that she was out in the yard with the baby in her arms.

Aloo's courageous act, and the malicious words that she had flung at the men, left them with the shame that demolished a man and reduced him to nothing. "All of you are cowardly women." They might have swallowed the words from the mouth of a man, but the naked words from a woman were unbearable. The men were angry. They even wanted to beat Aloo. Most of the men there were related to her. But then their mood changed. In place of anger Aloo's brave act inspired a new spirit in them. Aloo must not believe that she married among men who were more cowardly than women. Two men moved towards the door ready to enter the house. Others moved cautiously forward behind them. The sitting room was in a complete shambles. The chairs were broken and the main table stood on its hind legs with one side kissing the floor. The glass cupboard was shattered and most of the utensils were perched precariously on the wooden frame. There was much more damage than had appeared from the outside. At last two men entered the house, Ochieng, Aloo's distant brother-in-law, and Obwolo, Aloo's neighbour who was not actually related to her.

Ochieng stood timidly near the shattered glass cupboard, but Obwolo moved here and there unafraid. He was black, stout, and of considerable height. He looked much older than his actual age, but he was a brave youth with an air of dignity and pride. He had arrived on the scene soon after Aloo had rescued her baby from the house. Obwolo searched every corner of the house, carrying out to the yard any objects that looked suspicious. But the snake was nowhere to be seen.

The men who were searching the bedding in the yard announced that there was nothing there. Obwolo entered the bedroom again and searched it thoroughly. There was nothing. The people who stood away from the window shouted to him that perhaps the Satan had escaped through the wide gaps separating the roof from the walls. But Aloo refused to believe them. She moved towards the house and stood near the doorway shivering. If the snake were not found and killed, she would lock the door on all the mess and go to her husband at Ukwala Boma where he was the Divisional Police Inspector. She hated living alone in this village where the bush in the uncultivated land grew with furious determination during the wet season. Of course she could live permanently with Ojwang at Ukwala but then there would be no one to cultivate the land and to look after the numerous cows and chickens which supplemented the meagre earnings of her husband.

Meanwhile, as Obwolo was coming out of the bedroom, his eyes rested on a basket hanging on a club that was stuck on the thatched ceiling. He eyed the basket for a while. There was nothing unusual about its position. Many families hung their valuables in that way to keep them out of the children's reach. However, he had pulled everything else down, and there was no reason why he should not pull the basket down as well. He stood on one of the few unbroken chairs and clambered down with the heavy basket. Its weight was overwhelming. Obwolo felt that it probably contained nails, for Ojwang had been talking about building a new house. But if they were nails, there were surely enough to build several houses. Obwolo staggered with the basket towards the door where Aloo was standing. Aloo screamed in terror, "What have you got in that basket, Obwolo."

"That is what I want to know from you. It's a dead weight."

"It was empty this morning," Aloo screamed again.

"What!" Obwolo sent the basket flying towards the door. A horrifying feeling in his stomach made him quite sick. The basket with all its contents flopped in the doorway and a mighty snake emerged from it hissing in anger. At first it made straight for the yard where the people stood. Then it changed its mind. It unwound its coiled body and made for the broken table. Obwolo, was cornered at the end of the house with no door. The snake raised its head above the table. Its horrible forked tongue hypnotised Obwolo who felt as though he was nailed to the wall.

"The bedroom window! The bedroom window!" the crowd shouted themselves hoarse.

But Obwolo could not move, the door to the bedroom was much closer to the snake, which was heading straight for him. It was better to die where he stood than to go and meet it.

Then there was a terrific crash in the doorway. The snake turned its head sharply towards the door. There was nobody there. All that stood before it was the scattered countless pieces of a waterpot that someone had hurled in during the minute of confusion and panic. Obwolo stood behind the crowd wiping a bleeding cut that he had got as he miraculously wriggled through the small bedroom window. He was still breathing heavily. Never, since his childhood, had he been so close to death. The ghastly moment would haunt him for the rest of his life. The crowd gasped with joy when Obwolo leaped to safety and they turned to the monster. Sticks and stones were soon flying through the narrow doorway like hailstones during a storm. But the giant snake dodged them all, ducking its head below the missiles just in time. The yelling and cursing of the crowd disappeared into the distance leaving only the echo to mock back the frightful noise. One glance at the monster made new arrivals retreat in haste. It was as if Satan himself had descended from hell to bring death and decay to Kadibo village. Horror! The snake seemed to fill the house. Wherever you looked, it was there. Its forked tongue was like the flame of fire which fell upon the disciples on the day of the Pentecost. It moved restlessly in the house spitting furiously on the broken furniture, but never once did it move towards the doorway again.

The furious battle had raged for well over one hour. The men were getting anxious and growing more and more scared of the serpent and moving further and further away from the house. The nearest person to the house was now about ten yards away. The men were talking at the top of their voices and the scene was like a market place where you hear a lot of voices without catching a single word. Then one voice broke through the others, "Let Aloo call us women if she likes, but whoever gets near that Satan will not sleep in his hut again tonight."

"You are right," the crowd echoed.

"This snake has been sent by a ghost. You can tell by the way it has refused to leave the house."

In their confusion, the crowd did not miss Obwolo till they saw him running towards them. He had run to his home across the river on the other side of the hill where he had snatched up a bow and a sheath full of arrows. He moved past the crowd towards the door. The shouting crowd followed suit. Their shouts and shrieks aroused the snake's anger. It would fight for its life to the bitter end and would revenge itself on whoever dared to go near the house. It would certainly kill several of them before it was killed. It unwound its coiled body, revealing its full length with its head erect, and some people moved backwards trampling on their friends' toes. But Obwolo did not heed the shouts of the crowd.

He took aim at close range with one eye closed – he aimed, and re-aimed, and then let the arrow go.

The poisonous arrow went hissing through the air and the eyes of the crowd followed it with their breath caught in their chests. The giant snake ducked the arrow and moved its head violently to the right, but it miscalculated the direction of the arrow which landed squarely on its head. From afar it looked as if the arrow went right through its head. The monster quivered violently. Then it raised its head and struck furiously at the broken table, the only victim that was near. Then it raised its body in the air and crashed to the floor with a thud. "Its stomach has burst asunder," cried someone from the crowd.

The crowd surged towards the house, shouting and calling the names of all the medicine men they could think of. Women and children who had been standing well behind the men now wriggled between them to have a close look at the dead Satan. But their eagerness did not last. The supposedly dead snake sprang in the air and dashed out of the house as though possessed by the seven devils. The poison in its blood must have made it mad. The crowd scrambled dangerously to safety, and a handful of old men who were among them ran even faster than the others to save their lives. As Aloo said later, "Don't believe an old man when he says he is tired of living."

Within minutes, Aloo's yard was clear except for the heaps of stones and sticks that had been gathered to kill the monster. Behind the kitchen, Obwolo stood on the anthill still clutching his bow and sheath of arrows ready to shoot again if necessary.

But the serpent stood high in the air with its tail touching the ground and then it crashed heavily to the ground. It moved no more. It was dead.

For some time no one moved near it, but when Obwolo had examined the snake and pronounced it dead, the crowd moved nearer. The old men were bent double again, looking for their walking sticks which had been thrown away in the confusion.

The ugly dead serpent lay full length on the yard, its shiny black skin glittering in the midday sun. Aloo and her children stood behind the crowd. Something told her to abandon forever that house where the snake had moved about leaving its deadly saliva in each room. Kagonya was nothing but thick bush and green creepers during the wet season, yet the men did not make any effort to clear the areas close to the houses.

The crowd was just flogging the dead serpent when Ojwang arrived in unexpectedly, still wearing his police uniform. His appearance made Aloo sob and cry loudly, "How often have I pleaded with you to clear this bush around the home? I am not staying here tonight."

But Ojwang was not listening. He looked past his wife to the crowd that had gathered. Then his eyes rested on the dead serpent. The bad dream that had tormented him throughout the night started to reveal itself. He had dreamt that he attended two funerals in one day. He woke up unusually early, and when he had done the morning duties, he had asked for permission to come home.

They dragged the serpent away and buried it in a deep hole on the anthill.

The White Veil

"Sorry I am late Rapudo," she apologised calling him with his nickname that meant 'slim one'. "The children are doing exams and I had such a heap of marking to clear. I did not realise that it was so late." She slipped in beside him as usual. But instead of making room for her and patting her on the back as he usually did, he snapped at her.

"I am sick of listening to excuses about the children and the school. I always come second to your damn school and your children. I have been sitting here since 8.00 pm. It is now twenty past eight."

The waiter busied himself cleaning the table which did not need cleaning – Owila had only been in the bar for five minutes. He had seen him come in. Why was he lying to the girl he loved? The waiter looked at Owila and then moved to serve two Asians who wanted some beer.

Achola was taken aback. Her being late once in several weeks could not be the only cause of Owila's outburst. There must be something else. Only two days ago she had waited a whole hour for Owila in that very bar, and when he came panting, she had forgiven him with a smile and they had had a wonderful evening.

The waiter moved towards them again. "What would madam like?" he addressed Owila. "Water, please," Achola butted in. Owila did not protest or show interest. The waiter hesitated a little and then moved. He brought a glass of water and put it in front of Achola. They sat in silence for a while. Then Owila spoke without looking at her.

"I am getting tired of being pushed into second place all the time. I think I should give you time to attend to your school work. When you have made up your mind, we can make amends."

The words pierced Achola's heart. For a moment something blocked her throat completely and she could not breathe. She sniffed and the lump subsided as if she had swallowed it in her stomach and her bowels grew warm as if she wanted to go to the toilet. "What are you talking about, being in the second place, Rapudo? I have loved you and cared for you all my life. That you know – I don't have to tell you. If there is something else I swear I'll not take offence. Tell me!" She fumbled for a handkerchief in her bag to mop the flood of tears that was soiling her green blouse. But Owila was not looking at her.

"Anyway, I've come to the conclusion that you are not serious about me. We have known one another for five years now. You say you love me and each time I ask you for a thing that any man would ask from his fiancé you give lame excuses that cannot fill a basket. Other lovers do it, even some of my own friends. Yet I have to crave night after night because I am waiting to marry a virgin." He laughed mockingly.

"But, Rapudo, this is not the place for us to discuss such matters, let us go for a walk and discuss it. Please."

"No, we discuss anything right here," Owila cut in. "Others are busy having a good time, they will not care about us."

"But the waiters will hear us, Rapudo, please!'

"Forget them." Owila threw his hands in the air. "They can listen if they like."

"Rapudo," Achola said wearily, "if that's how you feel, then let's get married. It's you who wanted us to wait but if you've changed your mind now, I am ready too." She eyed Owila sideways as though there was some mistake, for the man sitting next to her was truly Owila but the words and the menacing voice were not his. The lights in the Rendezvous flickered green, blue, yellow and then returned to their normal dimness again.

"You have to be more sensible, Achola." For the first time in many years he now called her by her own name. He had always called her 'Ataye', her nickname. "Marriage is a long term thing; it will need time. I am talking about the immediate situation."

"But you have never spoken to me like that before, Rapudo. What has happened to you so suddenly that you now want us to break our promise? To spoil the wonderful moments we have shared all these years?"

"Well, I don't want to live in the past," Owila snapped. "I have just realised that I have been a big fool. You think you are more holy than Miss Hannington. Yet she spends the night in John's house quite often and she is a regular Sunday School teacher as well as being an ordinary teacher like you. And I bet that she is in John's house now. But you insist that we can only meet in a bar and when you come to the house you insist that you can't ..." He did not finish the sentence.

"I think you are being unfair to Miss Hannington, Rapudo. She may be spending the night there but I don't think she would misbehave."

"What do you mean by 'misbehave'?" Owila was angry. "John is a friend of mine. He himself tells me that you and me are just being ridiculous and old fashioned. He takes precautions and they cannot have a baby. I could do the same if you were sensible and willing to change your outmoded ideas."

Achola looked at her man unbelievingly. She had loved him passionately for a very long time. She lived for him and adored him. He had been a symbol of faith and an ideal man in her life, handsome, kind and holy. Now suddenly he spoke a sharp language that she could not understand. She felt helpless.

"But John and Miss Hannington are Europeans," she said, helplessly. "We cannot put our feet in their shoes. Moreover, their parents are not here. Nobody knows them here, so nobody will talk."

"That is exactly what I was telling you," Owila snapped again. "You are only interested in what people say. You don't care an ounce what I suffer." He was looking away from her. "Anyway, I have stated my case and I am through." He drained his glass and announced that he was sleepy and wanted to go to bed. Moreover the DC was going on safari tomorrow and he would have to relieve the DO 1. "I do most of his routine duties when he acts for the DC"

Achola sipped a little water. Her throat was bone dry. They got up and walked down the stairs in silence. The waiter watched them go. He knew them. He had seen them at the Rendezvous for many nights and he liked them because they were decent. Some silly couples send you for a drink, and when you bring it, you find them sucking each other's mouths. But these two only held hands. Sometimes he would put 'reserved' on their corner table when his instinct told him they would come. Tonight, as they stepped out of the hotel, he knew things were not well with them.

The streets were bright with lights. But Achola somehow felt lost and darkness was everywhere. She stumbled and nearly fell on the step separating the pavement from the main road. Owila stretched his hands and held her, saving her from falling. That was the only time their bodies came into contact and it was so brief. She stretched her hand out for him but he insisted that he must escort her back to the school. They walked on without talking. At the school gate they shook hands and parted.

Achola did not look back. She fumbled for her key and hurried towards her house. She was almost running. She located the keyhole and opened the door, closing it quickly afterwards. She switched on the lights. She ran her eyes round the room as though looking for something. Yes, there it was. She dashed towards it and grabbed it with both hands greedily. Her feet could not hold her any longer. She crumpled on her bed. She strained her eyes to looked at the life-size photograph that had stood at her bedside for a year. Yes, she was not dreaming. They sat side by side, with Owila's hands resting over her shoulder. Owila was a student at Yala Secondary School then, and she was in her final year at Ng' iya Girls School.

They had since taken several other photos, but somehow that one meant everything to her. It was taken the day Owila slipped the ring on her finger to crown the memories for their friendship and to warn other men that she was 'booked'. They were to marry as soon as she finished her Teacher Training Course. That same night after their engagement, when Owila was seeing her to her uncle's home, she had let him, for the first time, run his hands over her abdomen to feel the pimple-like tribal marks that had been incised on her body when she was a small girl.

"I didn't know your Christian parents would let you do this," he had told her.

Achola replied, giggling, "My grandmother took me secretly. She told me that mother was cheating me. All men including Christians liked a warm and appealing wife."

She stood still and let his hands touch the arched marks under her breasts too.

"All these!" he remarked, feeling good. "You must have endured a lot."

"Yes, it was very painful," she told him. "We stood in a row. The first one knelt before an old lady. She pierced the skin of the stomach with a thorn and slashed it off with a blade. She did the operation repeatedly according to our demands. She was a good old lady – she telling us that the more you have the more love you will get from your husband. So we knelt before her in great pain but still asking for more."

"I am proud of you," he had told her, while his hands lingered on the raised marks. Then he held her very tightly and crushed her to his chest. When she broke loose to go, he had stood there and watched her enter into her uncle's house. From that time their love had deepened. They had lived as one soul though with different bodies. Achola strained to look at the photo again but it was blurred now. A pool of tears had blotted out the two figures she had seen so clearly before. She wiped the photo and put it aside. She removed her dress but slept in her petticoat. She had no strength to do more.

A little sleep did come to her eyes but the naive remark that Owila had maliciously thrown at her, gnawed at her mind, John and Miss Hannington do it. We could do the same and I can use those things to stop us having a baby. The words were so painful that she did not want to think of them but they lingered on in her mind. A thought came to her. Maybe she had been a fool and old fashioned as Owila had told her. If that is what Owila wanted, if that is the only thing that could make her keep him, she would give in, perhaps once or twice. She would write to him tomorrow and apologise and offer to make amends. She buried her head on the pillow and slept.

Owila was in the office earlier than usual. He had had a restless night, and now a cracking headache hit him whenever the outgoing landrover doors were slammed shut. He looked at the pile of mail on his table, but his mind was not there. He walked across the room and took the little photo of Achola that stood in a hidden place over the filing cabinet. He looked thoughtfully at it, opened a drawer and put it there. Just then John walked in without knocking. John was a tall fair-haired Englishman. He was the youngest of the European administration in Nyanza and looked after Nyando Division. A bachelor, he lived in Mohamed Road, not far from the radio transmitters. He was good natured, unlike most of his people who were so withdrawn and cold. He was jovial and believed in life while he was young. John was only 26. His parents lived in the city of London and he had lived there all his life until he came to Kenya. He was friendly to Jenny Hannington, a teacher at Saints High School. He had not made up his mind to marry her, but for the time being they were having a good time.

The friendship between John and Owila developed when Owila was appointed DO in charge of the Winam Division. Owila was 25, only a year younger than John. They got on well. John had found the other Europeans at the station old and rigid in their outlook on life. They had warned him not to be too close to Africans or they would never obey him. But the young DO rebelled and chose his own friends.

Owila felt resentful to see John looking so fresh while he was nothing but a packet of misery. Last night when he walked sadly home from seeing Achola at her school he saw Jenny's car parked at John's door, and his heart ached. Perhaps John had walked in to boast or to tell him in detail what they had done. John never found it embarrassing to talk about sex to Owila – not because he was loose, but because he liked Owila and they were good friends.

"What is the long face for?" John asked at the door.

"Oh, I think old age is creeping up on me," Owila said, evasively. "I shivered all night. I think I have fever coming."

"Ha, ha," John teased him, "nothing to do with old age. You just need a woman to hug all night. That will overhaul your system completely. You have got a beautiful woman but you never invite her home. You are a fool not to have a good time."

Owila forced a feeble laugh and talked about something else to cover up the pain. If only John knew the number of times he had begged Achola to come and spend even part of the night in his house! But she would not agree because people would talk. He had given in to Achola's wishes because he loved her so much. They discussed some business for a while, and John left for safari. The examination started punctually at 9.00 o'clock. Achola could not eat any breakfast so she went to Standard Five and wrote all the questions on the blackboard long before the children came. At 9.00 o'clock sharp, she turned over the blackboard and read the questions to the children. It was a religious paper.

The last question read:

(a) Enumerate the 10 commandments.
(b) To whom did God give the 10 commandments?
(c) In which part of the Bible do you find them?

The children settled to their paper and Achola sat on a small table invigilating. Her swollen eyes ached from the bright light. She took a writing pad from her basket. She must write to Rapudo at once. She wrote a short letter telling Owila that she had thought over their talk, that she would consider his request and that she had had a miserable night. But when she re-read the letter her heart was uneasy. The answers listed on the pink paper before her stared at her. She read the answers to the last question. She did not want to. She tried to think of other things. Yet she found herself searching the lines till she found one of the Ten Commandments. – "Do Not Commit Adultery". She removed her eyes from the pages quickly – but the words haunted her. They were written everywhere she looked. She turned the paper upside down, but the words remained.

The folded letter stood before her. "What did adultery mean?" She racked her brain. Had she not heard the preacher say that it only meant sleeping with your brother's wife? Or was it not? She could not remember if the commandment also referred to sexual intercourse between a boy and a girl. Should she consult the Bible? It was just there before her. But she was too tired to bother. After all the language of the Bible was difficult, the tribal commandments were easier to remember and they were clearer. "A girl must be a virgin on the day of her marriage. This is the greatest honour she can bestow upon the man she is marrying and upon her parents." There was nothing to add to this. Achola was the first daughter, her mother was deeply respected – not only among Christians but among other women. Apiyo, the daughter of Ogo, her age sister who had married recently, brought great honour to her mother and her people when a bedsheet was returned to her home wrapped up in a goat skin. Her mother sat near the fireplace and other women powdered her with ashes because she had brought up her daughter well.

Achola took the letter and tore it into little bits and put the bits in her bag. She had made up her mind. It was all very well for Miss Hannington to give. But she was lucky because she was a European. Perhaps her people did not demand the bedsheet to be returned to the grandmother the day after the wedding.

Tears blinded her and she mopped her eyes. The children were busy with the examination. They would not see her. Something told her that Rapudo would come back to her without the high price he was demanding. No, the quarrel could not last. Rapudo knew full well that she would not live without him, she had refused all other men to wait for him while he was at school. Their friendship had lasted many years, and the numerous gifts they had exchanged was a clear indication to the world that they would eventually marry. Both parents knew about the friendship and they had raised no objection. All that was left was for Owila's people to approach her parents and start paying dowry. The children finished their Religious Knowledge paper and Achola went to the common room for a cup of tea.

On the fourth day after the row, a boy walked into Achola's house and handed her a letter in a blue envelope. She took the letter nervously and studied the handwriting for a while. The boy said no reply was needed and walked away. The letter was brief and simply written. There was no reference to the previous quarrel nor did it carry any message of love. It merely stated that Owila was going to a conference in Nairobi for a week and that on his return he would relieve Mr Wasigu, the DO Bondo Division, who was going to England for six months.

Achola read the letter again and again, each time hoping to isolate a single word that might comfort her. She moved restlessly about the house. She thought of many things. At last she sat down and hurriedly scribbled a short letter. It was not like her writing because she weighed each word again and again before putting it down. The letter read: "Rapudo, your letter has reached me. It has only partially lifted the shadow of sorrow that darkens my heart. I say partially because your handwriting has comforted me. But I yearn for the moment when I will see him whom I live for, whose heart lives in mine. Travel safely and return in peace."

She fingered the letter for a while, then she put it in an envelope and sent it to Owila's house through one of the school boys. "Do not wait for a reply," she told him. Then Achola sat on the verandah till she saw the boy running back to his class.

The busy examination time ceased and Achola had long miserable days and touchy sleepless nights that robbed her of the health and gaiety of youth. She had never known sorrow to this extent. She had been sick, sometimes she had been mistreated by her seniors when she first went to school, but never anything remotely like this. This was a kind of a sickness that was eating all her heart away, burying the past and blotting out the future she had so carefully planned. People who saw her walking thought she was alive, yet in her heart Achola knew she was a sick woman, moving in a big town among thousands of people without really seeing them. Yes, if Owila did not write, the sorrow was catching up with her, it would kill her.

One day, she bumped into John and Jenny at the market, "I haven't seen you for months," John greeted happily. "I hear Owila's doing very well in Bondo – he only complains of too much work. Have you been to visit him there yet?"

"Not yet," Achola said automatically. "I hope to visit him soon."

They looked busy and Achola felt happy when they said goodbye, greatly relieved that John had not asked her if Owila wrote at all. This was the first time that she bitterly learned that Owila was really in Bondo Division. Two months had slipped by with Achola looking in vain for Owila's letter. That night she dreamt that Rapudo had overturned his Landrover, and broken all his ribs. She rushed to the hospital to see him, but he did not recognise her. He was sweating heavily and his drying lips were peeling away and dry blood coloured his white teeth. Achola walked tearfully to the shops to buy him some orange squash. But on her return after barely half an hour, the nurse told her at the doorway that Owila had died. Achola woke up scared in perspiration and tears. She looked at her watch, it was just midnight. She slept no more.

Then the August holiday came and Achola was asked to go for a refresher course at Vihiga Teacher Training College for nearly one month. At first she told the headmaster that she was not well and wanted to go to her mother in Ugenya, but something told her to go to Vihiga. Hanging around Kisumu without Rapudo was useless. The evenings had become so dull and long she retired early each night only to weep. When she went home to see her mother for a few days before going to Vihiga, she avoided discussing Owila as she had in the past.

Vihiga Teacher Training College stood high in the rocky hills in Southern Maragoli. It was harvest time and the millet and maize planted in lines covered the entire ridges so that at dusk they looked like soldiers on parade. When the day's work was done, and the essays written, Achola went out climbing the ridges with a group of old schoolmates whom she had not seen for many years. They talked and laughed about their school days long past, and at sunset, they ran back to the College as the land was closing itself to sleep. Achola would stand at the gates of the College inhaling the evening air saturated with smells of roasting maize and the large unshelled local beans.

The change soothed somewhat Achola's yearning for Owila and she would even imagine that Owila had written and that letters were waiting for her at Kisumu. She ate and slept better and the country air slowly nursed her back to health.

When she returned to Kisumu the school was deserted except for the Opudo family who stayed there permanently during the holidays. Opudo's wife was a copy typist in town and her holidays never coincided with school holidays. Achola walked straight to their house to check if anybody had called to see her and if she had any letters.

"You look well, madam," Mrs Opudo greeted her gaily. "What were you eating at Vihiga? You've put on weight."

"Maragoli beans and sweet potatoes, and lots of fresh air."

"That's what I need," Mrs Opudo looked at her thin arms. "One needs a change from Kisumu. This hot air is draining all the oil from us leaving our young bodies ridged like old women!"

They laughed as they entered the house to have tea. Mrs Opudo told Achola about the things that had happened at Kisumu since she went away.

"Oh yes, and two women called to see you, and you have several letters here!"

She ran to the bedroom and returned with the mail. Achola took the mail; her heart was beating wildly as she wondered how many letters Owila had written and what they contained. Mrs

Opudo was talking to her, but she was not listening. She waded through the letters quickly. There was nothing from Owila. She looked at the envelopes all over again, not expecting a miracle, but to conceal the rushing tears, and to allow her eyes to focus properly. The hope that had lived with her during her course at Vihiga vanished. Three months had gone, a fourth month would start tomorrow, yet she had not heard from him. Achola thanked Mrs Opudo and left.

The church was full when Achola got there on Sunday. She usually sat with the choir, but today she entered unnoticed and sat at the back. She had no heart to sing – she only came to plead with God. He had given Owila to her to be her lover and future husband. Why had he taken him away? Why was he torturing her so? While the preacher preached a long sermon on repentance and the second coming of Christ, Achola was only half listening. When the sermon ended she wanted to slip away quietly before the usual announcements, but she was sitting in a corner, and to wade through the older women would attract attention. So she sat still, looking at the pulpit. Several announcements were made, then coming marriages were read:

"First I publish the Banns of Marriage between Solomon Ouma son of Manas Owira of Riwa Kisumu to Miss Ana Apiyo daughter of Ramogi, Seme. If any of you knows just cause or impediment why these two persons should not be joined together in holy matrimony, ye have to declare it. This is the second time of asking." The clergyman eyed the congregation critically, but there was nobody who raised any objection, so he signed the register. Then he raised his voice again. "The second marriage is between Absalom Owila, a son of Simeon Omoro, Siala, Nyakach to Miss Felomena Wariwa daughter of Oyoo of Usigu, Yimbo. If any of you knows just cause or impediment why these two persons should not be joined together in holy matrimony, ye have to declare it. This is the first time of asking."

Achola looked at the congregation and her eyes were dazed. Did they also hear what she had heard? She steadied herself a little because she could not breathe and could not hear her heart beating. The hymn book she was holding slipped from her sweaty hands and dropped between her feet. She looked at the pulpit, yes, the clergyman was looking at the congregation to see if anybody had any objection to the marriage between Absalom Owila and Felomena Wariwa. His hand was clutching a pen, yes, he was going to sign it. She must get up quickly and shout with all her strength. "He is mine. Owila is mine – Rapudo is mine…"

But she felt very dizzy and sick and she could not get up. The woman next to her held her hand. "My child, you have fever?"

Achola did not protest – she just leaned on the woman while the clergyman waded through numerous other announcements. When Achola gained her strength, people had started leaving the churchyard. The woman was still holding her hand. She decided quickly what to tell her. "Thank you mother – I felt suddenly sick, I think, I have malaria coming. I feel all right now, I will go home right away and swallow some quinine."

The woman looked at her – she had stopped sweating and she looked better.

"Go in peace, my child," the woman told her. Achola moved quietly from the church and walked straight home. She was surprised she reached the house safely, because she could not remember having crossed any road. Yet she must have followed the same dangerous road full of recklessly driven cars. She entered the house and ransacked the whole place. After about half an hour a heap of Owila's photographs lay piled high on a metal tray. Finally she brought the life-size one that stood near her bed and threw it on the heap without looking at it. The picture landed on the heap with the top facing upwards and the frame and glass intact.

Achola madly searched for a box of matches. She found it. She went to the store and brought out a tin of paraffin. She struggled to open the tin but it would not open. She put a cloth over it – still it would not open. Anger mounted in her; she threw the tin aside. She struck the match, it made a funny sound – the whole box was dripping wet and would not light. She had carelessly left it near the sink when she went to church and it had soaked up water. Achola stood with a wet match box in her hands staring at the heap of photographs before her. Then as if she had remembered something, she threw the matchbox away and grabbed the huge picture as if it were alive. She rubbed it violently on her chest, on her breasts, longing for the glass to break and pierce her heart: that was where Rapudo belonged. She was exhausted but she seemed possessed. She flopped on a chair, still clutching the photograph.

The afternoon was cool. People were walking towards the town. Sunday was a favourite day for sight-seeing and window-shopping in Kisumu. Young people from Nyalenda Village were laughing and talking at the top of their voices. They were coming towards her. She took a small path to avoid them. Some of them might be her students. Perhaps they would not recognise her. She had changed into a dirty old dress, she wore old slippers and she had covered her head and part of her face with a black scarf like a Nubian girl.

People were drinking and singing in the village. She mingled with the crowd that was walking towards the bar. She passed the first row of houses and the second. Where exactly was the house? Could she ask? No, she moved to the third row and turned into Odiaga Lane. That must be it, or at least it looked like it. A red tin roofed house with a white door. She gathered all her courage and knocked at the door. Presently the door opened and an elderly lady in a white gown stood before her.

"Come in, my child," the woman's voice was very soft. Achola lowered the cloth so that the woman could not see her face and followed her into the inner room which was spacious and lighter than the outer one. The lady sat on an easy chair. She took a small stool beside her and offered it to the visitor. Achola sat on it, her face was still covered and tears ran along her cheeks. The old lady moved close to her and removed the cloth from her face. The beauty and the tenderness of Achola's youth startled her. She had not had such a young customer for a very long time. She held Achola's face in her hands and searched her eyes pitifully.

"My child, what brings you to me at such a tender age?" Her voice was soft, almost a whisper. Achola opened her mouth to speak but her sobbing got louder till she could not listen.

"All right, weep as long as you like, when you finish, tell me your mission."

After a long time of weeping, Achola faced the old woman. "Now speak," the old woman looked away from her.

"I have lost the man I have loved all my life. I know I cannot live without him."

"Do you want to die then?"

"No, mother. I must not die because Rapudo, needs me. I want him to marry me. I want to live with him and look after him."

"But you have just told me that you have lost him. How can you marry him?"

"Mother," Achola burst out into tears again, "that is why I have come to you. Is there anything you can do?" Silence. Achola's eyes searched the older woman's face.

"How have you suddenly known that you have lost this man if you have loved him all your life?"

"I went to..." Achola stammered, now afraid to tell the old lady the truth.

"Carry on," the old lady encouraged her.

"In the church this morning, the clergyman announced that he is to marry another woman in three weeks' time. Oh mother, I nearly collapsed in the church. I wanted to stop him signing the register because Rapudo is mine, but by the time I had gained strength, he had signed it. We quarrelled one night four months ago, and a week later, he was transferred to Bondo Division. Though I have prayed daily he has never written to me, but I kept on hoping. Then today I got the shock."

"So you are a Christian?"

"Yes." Achola looked at her suspiciously.

"Will your parents be happy to know that you are here?"

"That I do not know, but I want you to help me, mother – that is why I am here. Please do not send me away."

"No, my child, I shall not send you away. I also work through God. I am his prophetess. He has given me power to see things that will happen and I am given the power to avert danger if I am warned in time. But many Christians do not believe in me. Yet they see my works daily."

"Mother," Achola looked at the prophetess eagerly, "do you think you can avert the wedding? Say you can do something to turn Rapudo's mind from this girl."

"But you have hardly given me enough time, my child. The wedding is already announced publicly. It will need drastic measures and quick action. But I want to be sure if you can keep a promise and if you can do exactly what I tell you."

"I will do everything you tell me, mother – anything that will make me marry Rapudo, not physically perhaps but if I can marry him in my heart that I may have something to live for."

"All right, I am willing to help you. Now tell me frankly why you quarrelled – that will help me in my work.'

"Mother, it was not a big thing," Achola said tearfully.

"However small, I must know."

"Well," Achola cleared her throat. "He wanted us to know each other before our marriage. But I would not, mother. I wanted to honour my mother." Achola hid her face from the old lady. Perhaps she had said too much. For a while the prophetess stroked Achola's neck. Then she lifted her eyes and spoke to her.

"Listen, my child, there is nothing to be sorry about. You are a noble woman. Unlike other educated women you have not taken to the white man's way. The God of our ancestors will reward you."

She brought out an old Bible from under the chair and placed it on her lap.

"Now put both hands over this," she told Achola.

Achola obeyed.

"Close your eyes."

Achola, obeyed.

"Say the words after me."

"I promise that I will strictly act on your word and that what we have discussed will remain a secret between the two of us. Amen."

Achola repeated the words after her. When she opened her eyes, the old lady smiled at her.

"Go in peace now. Come and see me after 19 days. When you come you will stay with me for 2 days. Tell no one where you are going. Should the headmaster press you, tell him that you are going to see your ailing mother. And remember keep your mouth shut and be back here on the 19th day."

As Achola left the prophetess's house she lowered the black cloth over her face so that nobody would recognise her. She hurried back to the school. The afternoon was far spent. She bathed and changed her clothes and, although she was not hungry, she forced down some food. A strange kind of peace flowed into her heart, a peace that she had not known for many weeks. Although the prophetess had not given her any sign of what she would do, somehow she trusted her. That night Achola slept soundly without weeping for Rapudo.

The school opened on Monday.

The last term was the busiest, with the countrywide examinations approaching. Achola threw herself wholeheartedly into work. The other members of staff had been told that Owila was to marry not Achola his longstanding girlfriend whom the whole school knew, but a girl from Yimbo Location. Knowing how much Achola loved Owila, none of them had the courage to ask her if she had heard the news. The weeks slipped by and Achola stayed out of church on Sundays. She pinned a calendar on top of her bed and each night before she went to sleep she put a cross over the figures to mark the end of a day.

The town was full of rumours about the coming wedding.

"What a beautiful girl for a man to leave," people said. Owila refused to discuss why he was jilting the girl like that to marry some girl from the bush whom he had only known for three months.

John and Jenny were upset to hear the news, but Owila refused to discuss why he was jilting the girl he had loved for so many years. Achola blocked her ears to rumours and avoided places where people could ask her awkward questions.

Then the 19th day of the month came. It was a Friday. After the morning lessons, Achola told the headmaster that she would be away for the weekend. Her mother was unwell and she would return on Monday by the early bus which passed near Pap Ndege School at 6 am. The headmaster gave her leave without further inquiries. In a way he was relieved to see Achola go out of town over the weekend. The staff had all been invited to the wedding and although they had blamed Owila for having dropped Achola most of them had accepted the invitation. To have Achola around at such a time would only be embarrassing.

By mid-afternoon Achola stood trembling at the prophetess's door. A black cloth covered her face. She did not mind what means the prophetess was going to use to avert the wedding, so long as Rapudo was safe to marry her one day. She had no particular thoughts about the other girl. She did not know her, she did not care for her and if she had allowed Rapudo to go to bed with her, then she was not worth ten cents or a wedding in the church.

The door opened unexpectedly and she went in. "I am glad you have kept your word," the prophetess told her.

"I always keep promises," Achola answered shyly.

The prophetess took Achola into a small bedroom which she told her would be hers while she stayed with her.

Have a little rest now. In the evening, I will talk to you." At 8.00 pm when supper had been served, the prophetess called Achola into her room to speak to her.

"Listen, my child. I want you to make a small present for Owila. I will tell you later how to get it to him. This is what I want you to sew for him."

She pulled out two white pillow cases which were richly embroidered on one side only.

"You are educated, I know you can sew. I want you to finish the work completely by tomorrow night before supper. On Sunday you and I will go on a long journey for a few days and when we come back from the journey, things will be different. Is that acceptable?"

"Yes, mother, I can do anything for him. I can start tonight."

"No, tonight you must sleep."

Achola was puzzled at the prophetess's arrangements. A numb feeling in her heart mocked her, seeming to tell her that the wedding would not be called off, but somehow the prophetess's face reassured her. She slept badly. Her nagging fears, coupled with the unusual surroundings made the night drag.

So Achola settled down and started sewing the following morning. She worked solidly without interruption except for a few minutes at lunch time. By supper two pillowcases were beautifully embroidered. Achola was exhausted and her fingers were numb from continuous sewing. Her neck was stiff, and a pain on her hack bothered her.

The older woman said, " Now have a bath and sleep. We are starting the journey early in the morning."

Achola was so exhausted that when she slept she did not even turn over. She woke up with a start when the prophetess tiptoed into her room.

"It is all right, I did not want to wake you early but you must move fast. First have a good bath then have your food – it is ready. When you finish, tell me."

Achola moved swiftly but quietly. She was now excited, but not the kind of excitement she had had before. Her mother came to her mind, and she lowered her eyes sadly. She knew her mother would not approve of her seeking the prophetess's advice. Yet she had gone too far now. She would go through with it and explain to her later. She was sitting at the edge of her bed when the prophetess called her. Achola followed her into her own bedroom. The door was shut. The prophetess turned and faced Achola.

"Promise once more you will do everything I tell you before we go on the journey."

"Mother, she burst into tears. I thought by now you would trust me."

"No room for tears, my child," the prophetess told her sternly. "Our journey will be very tedious. I must be sure." There was no trace of kindness on her face now, only hard business.

"I am sorry, mother. I will obey."

The prophetess then flung the door open and stood aside looking at her. Achola's heart stopped completely. If it was beating, she did not hear it. Little drops of perspiration formed over her nose and her forehead.

"Come," the prophetess beckoned her, but her feet were numb and heavy. She just started with her mouth open.

"Can I still trust you?" The prophetess asked her now with a smile.

"Yes ... mother." The words simply dropped out of her mouth.

"Then come; there is little time."

Achola dragged her weary legs into the room. The two bridesmaids stood aside fully dressed. A long bridal gown was spread over the prophetess's bed and its whiteness made Achola blink several times. The prophetess dressed Achola quickly while she stood like a statue. Her mind was completely blank. If she tried to think she would weep. The dress fitted her perfectly as if it was measured on her. Then the prophetess took the white veil and put it over her as all brides did. The part of the veil covering the front head had two layers. Then she slipped the bridal shoes onto Achola's feet

"Now listen, my child. The wedding is at 10.00 am. The car will get you to the church five minutes before the time. Nashon will go with you. Do not hesitate to enter. When you hear the sound of the organ walk gracefully towards the aisle. The groom will be waiting for you."

"But, mother, whom am I marrying?" Achola panicked. If the prophetess cheated her and fooled her to marry another man, she would break her Bible oath and die.

"You are marrying Owila." The prophetess gripped her hands – because they were trembling.

"I am marrying Owila," Achola said breathlessly. "But how, mother – what of the other bride?"

"I have planned everything perfectly. Kadimo is very far, my messenger told me that the bride was leaving her mother's house at 5.00 pm so as to be here by 9.00 am but they will not make it. It rained heavily on that side and the roads are very sticky. I can see them now, they are having a bad time on the road. By the time she arrives the ceremony will be almost through."

Achola's hands had not stopped trembling – she had tried to imagine the whole plan, but fear stopped her.

"But Rapudo will recognise me mother, and then ... and then ...."

"Just trust in me. Owila will not recognise you till after the ceremony. Then even if he does not want to marry you physically you will be married to him in your heart. You will be bound to him. Now forget about the other girl and only think about yourself. My heart will go with you."

The two black cars stood waiting adorned with flowers. People standing by assumed that this was just another bride going to meet her man. They had seen so many bridal cars and there was nothing unusual about it.

Achola was helped into the first car by the man called Nashon. The little bridesmaids sat with her, one on each side each holding a little white bouquet. The prophetess stood at the door with her hands clasped over her chest. Achola caught a glimpse of her through her double veil and her heart felt at peace. Then the cars moved away.

St. Peter's Church was packed with friends and relatives of the bride and groom. Two candles were burning brightly at the altar. Reverend Omach and Father Hussen stood wearing their white and black robes. The groom with his best man stood in front with white flowers in their button holes. The congregation sat quietly listening to the soft organ music. Owila was a little nervous – he had had a hectic week with numerous arrangements to make. The District Commissioner had given him 10 days off as part of his holidays. He would make use of those 10 days to know his wife better, because quite frankly, things had happened so hurriedly that he had not had a chance to know her well.

The few people who were still talking outside the church rushed in to find their places and the whispers filled the church. "The bride has arrived."

As the bride stepped into the entrance of the church the organ boomed out, "Here comes the bride," and the people got up to honour the bride and her maids. Achola walked gracefully towards the aisle. Owila had turned round and now found her. The sight of him nearly made Achola topple over; she had not seen him for four months. Her heart ached so much that she felt something wet running about her cheeks.

"No, Owila could never belong to that other woman. He is mine." Owila had met her, they were standing side by side now. Then they walked up the aisle following Reverend Omach who led them. Achola felt Owila's shoulders rubbing against hers as they knelt together on the cushions before Father Hussen. Old memories filled her heart strengthening her to go through with it.

The hymn ended and Father Hussen's voice filled the church and the solemn swearing of, "Will thou have this woman to be thy wedded wife" started.

Achola listened to the words attentively, but her heart was drumming away in her ears at the thought that soon Father Hussen would call upon her to repeat those very words and Owila might recognise her voice. She gripped hard on the rail to stop her hands from trembling. She heard Owila's voice saying, "I will," and then Father Hussen, faced her. "You, Felomena

Wariwa, wilt thou have this man to be thy wedded husband?" Achola swallowed and then said faintly, "I will."

A cold breeze swept through the church. The congregation was attentive. Some of the couples who had been married for many years listened to these strange words from the priest with renewed passion. Jenny Hannington pressed John's hand and whispered, "I can't wait to see this woman's face, I am dying to set my eyes on her. I suppose she is very beautiful to have swept Owila off his feet just like that."

"Well, people around Kisumu know very little about her. I bet they are all dying to see her."

They say she is just from the bush, no roads, no shops and yet, John, she is so beautifully dressed and carries herself like a Queen."

"I don't care, Jenny, I think the other woman whom Owila jilted is a star." John strained his eyes at the crowd not really expecting to see Achola there, just restless. Then he whispered to Jenny, "She can't be here, she must be so broken-hearted."

Owila hesitated as he pronounced the words, "till death do us part." He had always felt that Christian marriage was committing a man too far, but he suppressed the thought. So many other men had gone through the ordeal. Maybe a new generation will revise the prayer-book and leave these words "till death" out. He let go the bride's hand, and on the direction of Father Hussen, Achola took Owila's right hand in her right hand and repeated the same words after Father Hussen.

"I Felomena Wariwa take thee Absalom Owila to be my wedded husband."

Achola's faint voice trembled away as she struggled to say the words after Father Hussen, Owila just managed to hear the words, but that satisfied him. He as a man had found those words heavy and strenuous to say so he could not blame his bride for being afraid. Then the ring was placed on the book of God for the blessing. Father Hussen took the ring and gave it to Owila and asked him to place it on the fourth finger of the bride's left hand. Owila held the ring tenderly and followed the words:

"With this ring I thee wed, with my body, I thee worship and with my worldly goods I thee endow. In the name of the Father and of the son and of the Holy Ghost. Amen!"

Owila felt hot under the arms and could feel the perspiration pouring down on his side. Was he afraid? No, he was just excited. To get married and to wade through all these ominous words was not easy. A devilish mask of Achola, the girl whom he once loved so much flashed through his mind appeared without a warning, and the perspiration under his arm increased, but he shook her out of his mind. He was a married man now and when in the arms of his bride, he would forget Achola completely. Yes, it was just a matter of time. Then Father Hussen pronounced:

"These whom God has joined together let no man put asunder." And Father Hussen eyed the congregation critically and told them, "For as much as Absalom and Felomena have consented together in holy wedlock and have witnessed the same before God and this company, and thereto have pledged their troth either to other, and have declared the same by giving and receiving of a ring and by joining of hands, I pronounce that they be Man and Wife together, in the name of the Father and of the Son and of the Holy Ghost. Amen."

But Father Hussen's last words were drowned by a murmuring that broke out from the congregation. Father Hussen adjusted his glasses to focus and his eyes rested on the Reverend Omach's open mouth. A bride and twelve bridesmaids were walking along the path towards the aisle. Yes, they were halfway along the aisle. The congregation was now out of control and all talking loudly.

A woman's voice called, "Can't someone do something?"

Another voice shouted, "There must be a mistake."

The growing confusion brought the bridal procession to a halt. Father Hussen stood at the altar shouting at the top of his voice, "Order, Order! My children, Order!"

The congregation responded to his trembling voice and there was silence in the church. Father Hussen then walked towards the bridal party. He stood before the bride and asked her aloud, "My daughter, you must be in the wrong place. We are in the middle of another wedding. And whom are you marrying, my daughter?"

"Absalom Owila."

The shrill emotional bridal voice echoed through the church, and the people who sat in the front pew heard the words quite distinctly. For a minute or so there was dead silence. Then an insistent murmuring broke out again in the congregation. Father Hussen walked back to the altar where Owila was still kneeling besides his bride. He removed the double veil from the bride's face and Owila came face to face with the girl who had just been proclaimed his wife. Owila disentangled his arm from the woman kneeling besides him. Either he was dreaming or he had gone off his head. Achola's tearful eyes were fixed on him.

"But Father, Father ..." Owila staggered to his feet.

"She is not my bride. She is ..." And Owila turned round to face the congregation and there before him stood Felomena – the girl he was supposed to marry, with her bridesmaids. He staggered down to her, but Father Hussen barred his way.

"My son, you cannot go to her and leave your wife here. You are married to this woman now!"

"No, no, no," Owila shouted. "Do something, Father, please."

"Not now, my son, the solemn promise you had both said to one another is binding."

The congregation was out of control again. Some were shouting, others were weeping around the woman who had fainted before them. Owila turned round to look at Achola but the woman in the white bridal gown was nowhere to be seen. He broke loose and hurried towards the crowd but they barred his way and he could not see Felomena or her bridesmaids. He shouted to them to give him way. But his voice was drowned by the crowd, like a man cut off from help in a nightmare.

At the altar Achola was sobbing before Father Hussen. "He is mine. I have loved him all my life – I will serve him all my life. He is mine." And Father Hussen went down and tapped on Owila's shoulder.

"My son, your wife is waiting for you."

Land Without Thunder

The Lake shore was still deserted. The water looked swollen and angry as though it would swallow up the land and all its inhabitants. Frogs, crickets and fishing birds called sorrowfully at their mates. Half the sun had risen above the water's surface, and one could see a long stretch of the lake shore till it narrowed down at the tight neck of the land that separated the people of Agok from the clan of Naya.

Fear chilled Owila's mind. It was already light yet there were no other fishermen in the vicinity. He glanced at his cousins searchingly – they were busy untying the knots on their fishing nets, and there was nothing on their faces to raise an alarm. Owila slowly glanced homewards. The whole land seemed at peace. There was not even smoke curling above the euphorbia fences to show that women were preparing their morning meal.

Owila bundled the nets together nervously and threw them into the canoe before him. Something was wrong. A paralysing chill ran through Owila's whole being and settled in his stomach below his navel. But Owila had no courage to tell his cousins that the lake looked swollen and fearful and that Agok looked mournful. To cast doubt in the minds of people going fishing in mighty waters was like casting doubt in the minds of men going to war. Such an offence was punishable by death. He bit his lips. What was he afraid of? He was the healthiest and the strongest of the two cousins. They all accepted him as the brains of their group. The cousins filled their mouths with handfuls of water. Then they spat the water out, first towards the sun and then towards land. They pulled out their oars and eased the canoe into the water. Owila inhaled fresh air a couple of times. The early morning lake breeze and the whispers in the waves held the secrets of his youth. He had been only ten years old when his uncle came to take him to attend school in town. Owila had already refused to enrol at a local primary school only six miles from home. But when his father called him and told him that being the eldest son he had the first choice of the education his uncle was offering the family, Owila rebelled. He was not interested in schooling. He disappeared from home for two days and returned when his uncle had gone. After turning down the offer to go to school Owila's desire for the lake grew. He left the herding of cattle in his brother's hands, and accompanied his father to learn the tricks of fishing. It was the right choice, he knew it. He and his cousins had fished together since they were children. Fishing was the only occupation he knew, he would stick to it all his life, and in old age hand his oars to his son.

Owila's thoughts were interrupted by a strong wind that started suddenly from the mainland. It approached the lake hissing mightily like a whirlwind.

The morning looks rough, my brother," said Obuya first. "Tighten your oars and let's sail towards Naya shore, to avoid the wind."

"You are right," the men echoed together. They changed places so that Owila and Ochuonyo, took the top part of the canoe: their hands were firm and swift at the paddles. Obuya took his place after he knew the men would rely on his orders as they always did when there was trouble. Though older, Obuya was small. He was not handsome but his deep rich voice gave him a natural air of superiority and bred confidence among his relatives. Maybe it was his authoritative voice that made him marry a tall plump wife who mothered him. This day Owila detected an indefinable note of uncertainty in Obuya's voice and his hand trembled as he gripped the oars more tightly with both hands. Yes, this was the uncertainty he had felt while they worked on their nets. For ten minutes the cousins battled furiously to guide the little canoe towards the Naya shore, but it stubbornly faced the unknown destination. And when the cousins eased their paddles for a minute to gain breath, the canoe sped away towards the middle of the lake as if some powerful hands were propelling it away by force from the land of Agok.

Then Owila's eyes rested on a thick black cloud that was collecting over the clan of Agok. The entire land looked as dark as if night was approaching, and the darkness was extending rapidly towards the lake.

"Raise the alarm! Someone please raise the alarm! Look, it is going to rain mightily, turn your eyes towards Agok and see!" But Owila's warning came too late. Obuya fumbled at the side pocket of the boat; he found the white cloth, tied it on a stick and waved it furiously above his head to attract other fishermen. But there was no other canoe in the vicinity. In no time the thick clouds had reached the lake shore, with a furiously seething wind, and the lake became wavy and rough. The canoe moved forwards then backwards and then swerved dangerously sideways. Obuya yelled to his cousin, "Paddle no more! Let us preserve our strength – we may have a long way to swim."

But Obuya's words were drowned by the hissing sound of the tremendous storm that now started to fall. The canoe became wild. The cousins let it drift where it wanted, while they battled to shovel away the hailstones that rapidly filled it. Ochuonyo, who had so far kept quiet cried out: "What have we done to the ancestors that they should deny us the warmth of our huts?" He threw the calabash down and wiped water and hailstones from his head. "What are you doing, Ochuonyo? Shovel the hailstones!"

But Obuya replied, "I am jumping out." He had tied a rope around his waist and his eyes looked terrifying. "I am returning to my wife and my child, they need me."

The echo of his trembling voice was picked up by the hissing wind so that his voice returned as though someone was repeating his words.

"You are not jumping out," Owila grabbed his arm carelessly.

"We have lost our direction – you cannot swim ashore not knowing where you are going. You remain here. We survive or perish together."

But Obuya pulled away from Owila crying wildly, "I am returning home, they need me." He threw his oar away. As he made to jump out, Owila grabbed his arms. The two men lost their balance, slid on the slippery hailstones that filled the canoe and crashed down together in a heap. Ochuonyo grabbed his oar to steady the canoe, but the canoe capsized. The men scrambled for the sides of the slippery boat, screaming and calling on the forefathers long gone. Owila miraculously perched himself on top of the boat. Someone was clinging to his legs, and powerful hands were tearing his flesh away from the canoe. But he held the sides of the canoe firmly with both hands. He would not let go till his two arms fell out of their sockets. A hand that had grabbed the side of the boat near his was no longer there. Hailstones were still falling. He could see nothing. Then Owila heard cries and shouts. Someone was calling his name but the words were not distinct, and when he shook water from his ears, the flimsy voices died away and he heard them no more.

The hailstones continued to fall on Owila's back. His head ached desperately. Salty respiration blended storm-water dribbled from his head and was carried away by the powerful waves. After what seemed like many hours of torture, he opened his eyes. The hailstorm had stopped. The sun must have been above his head because its sparkling reflection on the water blinded him. The capsized boat was drifting aimlessly in the water. His numb lifeless hands were still clinging to the edges of the canoe as if they were nailed there. His legs? They were still there. The hands that had clung to them tightly for so long were no longer there, although they had left stinging bruises around his ankles. He suppressed the thought of what might have happened to his cousins. Their fate would be his too. It was just a matter of time. "We survive or perish together," he had told Obuya just before the canoe capsized.

Owila thought of his wife Apiyo, beautiful, young and devoted.

When prophets foretold that the lake was rough and thirsty for human blood, Apiyo had pleaded with Owila not to go fishing. Such warnings in Uyoma never passed without incident. But Owila, like many other fishermen in Agok did not heed the prophets' warning. He offered a small sacrifice to the ancestors to avert the misfortune onto someone else. Owila wished he had listened to his wife, but how could he? The cousins respected the views of one another more than those of their wives. The only obstacle between them was Awino, the wife of Obuya, who had only one child, a daughter. It was perhaps the craving for another child, a son perhaps, that made her intensely jealous of the other three couples, and she accused them of having 'tied her womb'. Many a time her husband comforted her. "There are many couples who have no children while God gave us one to cover our nakedness."

But Awino remained adamant, always looking for an opportunity to have a row with her sisters-in-law and a chance to tell them that they were boastful because they had houses full of children while she had nothing but a single eye.

When evening came, the scorching sun was replaced by a bitter cold that chilled Owila's body to the bone. His limbs had been nibbled by the lake creatures and were numb and lifeless so that he felt no more pain. Days and nights succeeded one another in long spells that stretched out like a whole season of the year. When the sun shone, it was like carrying hot bricks on the back, and the deadly chill of the nights blotted every thought out of Owila's mind. It was better to die, to rest eternally. Yet the thin thread on which Owila's life hung refused to break. Now and again he let his tongue hang in the water, and the little sips he caught cooled his burning throat.

Owila was picked up by some fishermen about 10 miles from the shore of Agok on the fourth morning. They lowered his battered body gently into their canoe and sailed to Agok shore. Almost the entire clan were still gathered at the lake shore. When the crowd saw the foreigner's boat sailing towards them they knew that the body of their son had been picked up and was being brought home. The wailing of the women rose to the sky and the men moaned and chanted. "One funeral is bad enough but to have three together from a small clan like Agok is a terrifying catastrophe. The new year will surely be rough for our people."

Owila's wife fell on her face on the muddy earth, afraid to set eyes on the body of her husband. Could God not have been a little kinder to her? She was an orphan. She had known nothing but starvation and suffering when both of her parents died. But when she married Owila and had her own children, the sore wound in her heart healed completely, leaving no trace of a scar because Owila loved her so. The six happy years of her marriage with Owila were dead; she was an orphan all over again.

The crowd pressed forward towards the boat. A man with an unfamiliar voice shouted to the crowd.

"Peace, my brethren, let us lower your son out of the boat." But the crowd did not heed. They surrounded the canoe and dragged it onto the dry land. Owila sat supported by one man at the tail of the boat. When the crowd set eyes on him alive, their cries redoubled and there was a panic as if a man long dead had opened his eyes and smiled to the mourners. Omach broke loose from the crowd and ran to his mother.

"Mama, mama, baba is back – he is sitting in the boat, come and see." But Apiyo pushed her son away. "You are young, my son, you don't understand, your father is dead, let me moan."

"He is not dead, mama, he saw me." Apiyo listened. The wailing and chanting had died down and groups of people thronged the boat speaking in low voices. She got up trembling and pushed her way through the crowd. Before she could gather enough courage, her eyes rested squarely on Owila sitting up in the boat, alive! She leaned on the boat close to him, and their eyes met. Owila was still alive. She staggered away from the crowd and sat on debris of an old canoe nearby. She was not thinking, she was just exhausted and frightened. Then Owila asked his people in a low voice, "What is news of my brothers?"

But instead of replying the wailing and chanting rose again, and the people mourned for a long while. Then an old man told Owila, "Look up there under that tree, the bodies of your cousins lie there in peace."

Owila's eyes followed the direction of the old man's hands till his eyes rested on the two new graves. He covered his face and sobbed aloud and his manly voice was drowned by the wailing of women.

They made a stretcher, and carried Owila home, following the familiar path he had walked on with his cousins from childhood days. His cousins were being abandoned at the lake shore to lie there for ever. Their souls would bathe in the morning breeze, and listen to the lullaby of the laughing waves. Confused thoughts span and whirled in Owila's head as his bearers turned their back on the water and he swore under his breath never to return to the lake.

As they walked home, Apiyo saw Obuya's wife eyeing her with intense jealousy, and Apiyo knew she hated Owila to have survived while her husband drowned. Apiyo lowered her head and walked away. God had blessed her above other women. Owila was alive. The relatives bathed Owila's battered body and soaked his nibbled feet in medicine prepared from the dry bark. Then his body and soul were purified from the tragedy he had witnessed. When darkness fell they returned to their homes leaving Apiyo to care for her husband.

Then Owila told his wife how when they had gone a few yards they saw the dark clouds covering Agok completely. Within a few minutes the wind and the hailstorm hit the canoe and it capsized. "How I got on top of that canoe is a mystery to me, and if I had not been picked up today, I would have died."

"Owila carefully avoided telling his wife of the terrible moment when Obuya announced that he was jumping out of the canoe to return to his wife and children because they needed him. He did not tell her about the powerful hands that had gripped his legs and the terrifying voices that called him. No, he would tuck those sad memories right in his heart till he met his cousins in the land of the dead.

"I am tired, Apiyo. Let me sleep now, there is tomorrow, we can talk then."

"It is a miracle that you are alive, sleep now," she told him. Apiyo covered her husband and her arm made a warm cushion under his head.

A wave of powerful sleep came upon Owila, and he did not resist it. Then he tossed his head restlessly. Was Apiyo calling him? He put his head on Apiyo's arm again, the faint voices came again more distinctly and aggressively. The powerful hands started to shake him out of the sweet sleep.

"Owila, Owila, wake up, are you not going fishing with us today? The sun is up in the sky, wake up, wake up." Owila woke up with a start and sat upright. He was groaning like a man being strangled and a choking sound came from his mouth.

Apiyo got up trembling. "What is it, Owila, what is it?"

"They are dragging me up," Owila stammered. "They were dragging me to go fishing with them. Oh, Apiyo, it was terrible, each one of them pleading and calling my name."

"Hush, Owila," Apiyo comforted her husband. "It's a bad dream – you have suffered so. Lie down and try to sleep. I will keep awake and watch."

Owila obeyed his wife and slept, and Apiyo tucked him in pulling a blanket up to his neck. She lay down near him, still trembling.

"They were dragging me up." Apiyo could not dare ask who they were. Who else could they be? If Owila had imagined or dreamt about those men, it was the beginning of serious trouble. But before she could close her eyes to sleep, Owila screamed and sat upright. "They are dragging me towards the lake by force. Apiyo, I tell them I no longer want to go fishing, but they insist I must go with them."

And Owila sat there sobbing.

"Light the lamp, Apiyo, they are here in the room. Tell them to leave me alone, I have given up fishing, tell them, tell them."

Apiyo threw her arms around her husband protectively. "They cannot be here," she wept. "Your cousins lie in their graves at the lakeside. You are imagining things Owila, lie down and rest, you are exhausted."

But Owila did not lie down and the darkness scared him. When Apiyo lit the little oil lamp and made the fire, Owila's eyes darted from corner to corner to make sure that the three men were not in the room. Then he announced to his wife, "I am not lying down any more, they will come back again!"

With a deep sigh Apiyo remembered how Obuya's wife had eyed her when they separated at the gate, and she remembered how her strength waned away when she set eyes on Owila in the boat. Yes, it was not only the three widows who were jealous of her, the men were jealous too. Why should Owila keep warm in his hut while they lay abandoned at the lake shore?

Owila's father was called from the main village at dawn, and when he heard the words from his son he said, "What do they want from you, my son? They have gone where we will all go." He spat on the floor and left to consult the wise men among his people for the well-being of his son.

That afternoon, two main cleansing ceremonies were done to keep the spirits of the dead men away from Owila's hut. But when night came, and Owila fell asleep, the voices again came, sometimes pleading, sometimes shouting, sometimes threatening. The images of the two dead men formed wherever Owila looked, and their whispering voices became a continuous whirring sound that tormented him out of sanity. At the end of the first week, an old medicine woman from Kajulu near Kisumu made a journey down to Agok at land's end. The blood of a pure white goat was shed. The goat's skin was treated with care and then trimmed into thin long straps. While the skin was still wet, the strips were twisted singly and knotted at the ends. Then the strips were bundled together and tied at one end, leaving the other end loose. The whole paraphernalia looked like a fly whisk made of strings. It was then smeared with pounded herbs mixed with oil and hung on a new wooden peg on the wall so that the strips dangled over Owila's head. The old woman then knelt near Owila's bed and whispered to him, "From now on they will not come in this hut; they belong to the lake, they must rest there."

That day, Owila slept till sunset, unmolested, and the peace of mind he had not known for so long returned to him. When night came, he ate with a wonderful appetite and slept without a stir the whole night. Owila whispered his gratitude to God and to the ancestors, and the Agok people marvelled at the powerful hand of the old medicine woman from Kajulu who had pacified Owila's mind. That morning, when Apiyo went to fetch water she studied the pond carefully before dipping her pot in the water to fill it. The reflection of her face stared back at her, moving rhythmically with the gentle tide. She drew water with the little calabash, filled her mouth and then spat it towards the sunrise.

"*Thu!* May we have peace in the family, today and forever, may Owila's health be assured!"

She filled her water pot and hurried home. The early morning sun looked kind and composed before her, it had a message of peace and prosperity. While she fixed her eyes on the sun a greyish cloud in the shape of a limbless man raced over the sun in the opposite direction. It seemed to be the only one in a clear blue sky. Apiyo did not like it but her eyes seemed to follow its movements wherever it went. She reached home to find Owila talking to relatives who had come to wish him long life.

Because the visitors hinted that they were hungry, Apiyo busied herself making the midday meal. Owila's father sat with two old men under the eucalyptus tree talking in low voices. Suddenly it started to drizzle, then there was a startling lightning followed by a roaring thunder. Owila's hut was struck by the lightning. The agonising yell of the men was heard in the neighbouring huts, and people rushed to Owila's hut to save them. But when they entered the hut, they found Owila and the visitors dumbfounded but alive! Only one thing was missing – the strips of the goat skin that hung over Owila's bed were no longer there, even the wooden peg had been taken away by the lightning. The rain stopped as suddenly as it had come. Owila sat still, and for some minutes he thought the blood had frozen in his veins. And when Apiyo rushed and threw her hands around him, he was not aware of her. He stared blankly into space, dazed by yet another narrow escape. Faintly, like the whispering waves of the lake, the voices returned to Owila's hut to molest him. Then, one by one, the visitors spat on the floor and left, *"Tho, tho,* we have never seen such a thing."

Left alone, Owila's father stood at the door of his hut perplexed about the kindness of God the Creator. He had kept Owila alive for four days in the mighty waters when his cousins drowned – why then was he allowing their spirits to return to the village to molest the people, who had offered numerous sacrifices to appease them? Owila's father looked at the mighty waters only a mile or so from his hut, and the rushing waves hitting the lake shore *waa-waa-waa.* Then the whole land started talking, "The lightning has snatched medicine from Owila's head," and the whole clan was shaken, not knowing what would come next. But no medicine man in Uyoma wanted to be involved in this complex situation. They all advised that the old woman should be called back. So they sent for her.

As if she was aware of what might happen, the old woman, when she returned, told the family calmly, "There is no thunderstorm in Mombasa. Owila must travel there immediately before the worst comes upon him." The family did not accept the old woman's decision. Owila was not in a state to travel. But the woman would not hear of it. She prepared another bundle of strips of skin and sewed it up in a new papyrus kikapu, ready for the journey. At first Owila also refused to go but his hut became unbearable. Going to Mombasa was an escape from Agok, the people, the lake and from the spirits of his cousins. Accompanied by Ogalo his cousin, he blindly caught the Mombasa-bound train at Kisumu, fifty miles from Agok. He left Apiyo weeping.

Owila's unexpected visit caused a stir among Agok people living in Mombasa. The word spread round and people asked one another, "What is it that brings him here while Agok is still mourning his cousins?" So, long before sunset, Ogalo's house was full of anxious looking relatives who had come to hear about Owila's unusual visit. When food and drinks were served, Ogalo addressed his clansmen and gave them the message of the clan elder who instructed him to tell Oyugi and the others why they had decided to send Owila to Mombasa while the land was still mourning his cousins. Then Ogalo lowered his voice and told his relatives how lightning struck the hut during a shower and snatched the medicine and the wooden peg from the wall above Owila's head. The medicine woman was called back and she suggested that if Owila was brought to Mombasa where there is no thunder, he would recover.

To the relatives gathered there, Ogalo's lengthy speech was just like one of those tales the older folk told the children around the fire after the evening meal. Yet it could not be a tale, because Owila sat before them in person.

Oyugi cleared his throat to conceal the fear that froze up his heart. Of course the rains in Mombasa were silent, but how could he be sure that another miracle couldn't happen? If the spirits were determined to get Owila's medicine again they would get it at any cost. But he was afraid to tell Owila, so he found himself saying, "We cannot doubt the voice of the clan. Owila is our blood. His trouble is ours." Then all the Agok people assembled to pledge their support to help Oyugi as long as the visitors stayed with him. Owila could not keep back his tears when he told his relatives about the lake disaster and about the voices. Women who sat in the room were sobbing quietly. To be haunted by the spirits was worse than death itself. In a way they were eating Owila's body and soul away till nothing would be left of him.

At bedtime, the *kikapu* was slit open and strips of goat skin were taken out and hung up above Owila's head as the old medicine woman had instructed them. But Oyugi could not stop trembling. Owila's junk of skins frightened him.

Owila tossed his head restlessly on the hard grass pillow. He could hear Ogalo snoring in the front room. The small green underpants that he wore clung like a glove on his moist thighs. A blanket lay in heaps under his feet. He glanced cautiously at the dangling strips of skin which were still there hanging above his head. Then he turned his head on one side to nurse sleep. Perspiration was streaking from his head down his face and his neck, and a small pond of salty water collected in the grove between his mammary glands. He dabbed the sweat with a cloth but it collected again. The air was humid and still, and there was not enough saliva to moisten his lips.

Outside the sound of the mighty sea could be heard like the sound of boiling water in a covered pot. Owila wondered how long he would last in this land without thunder. He had wanted to tell the elders that he preferred to remain in his hut in Agok under the care of his affectionate wife but he was afraid of them. The room was slightly darker now because the moon had retired. Owila slept as the early sea breeze filled the hut. Once more, Owila was grateful to God and to the ancestors, for his disturbed mind improved enormously on his arrival in Mombasa, and the voices disappeared completely. He bathed and ate, and even shared jokes with relatives, but his freedom was checked when he overheard Oyugi's wife complaining, "Other women have all the time in their hands, while I am stuck up in the house entertaining all day long."

Oyugi had replied humbly, "But he is only a visitor, he will soon return home."

"I am reaching my limit," she grumbled. "And when I do you'll bring someone else to cook."

Owila had noticed on the first day that Oyugi's wife did not like him, but he was desperate. He swallowed his pride and turned a deaf ear to her grumbles.

Then Oyugi's children fell seriously sick only five days after Owila's arrival at their home. Day and night they screamed that someone was strangling them, and no medicine cooled their burning flesh. And Oyugi's wife, Ambajo, became hysterical. "Take the medicine away from my house. I cannot bury two sons in one day."

"But Owila's medicine has nothing to do with the children's illness," Oyugi whispered to his wife. "You only want to use this chance to turn Owila out, Ambajo. It was the clan elders' decision!"

"Take the medicine away from my house," Ambajo yelled.

"The clan elders have houses full of children, why should they wipe my name from the face of the earth, why should they?"

"Ambajo, please, be reasonable. Look at it this way ..."

"Take the medicine away from my house," and her voice shattered the slums of Makupa village.

"There are so many Agok people living in Mombasa, why did God pick on me?" Ambajo was determined to talk her husband into expelling Owila from the house, but Oyugi walked away. He took the short cut to Makuti where some of his people lived, to talk things over. Of course he could not dismiss his wife's fear that it was Owila's medicine that had struck his house with disease. But Ambajo's language was calculated to embarrass him before his cousins, and his clansmen.

Oyugi found the two old men he wanted drinking palm wine under a coconut tree. When he told them that his only children lay dying with fever, they asked him, "What type of fever?"

"They are screaming that someone is strangling them,"

"Owila's cousins are angry with you," one old man told Oyugi bluntly. "They were bound to revenge sooner or later. Let Owila return to his hut and appease the spirits of his cousins."

Oyugi's knees shook where he sat. He did not like Owila's type of illness, nor did he like the look of Owila's paraphernalia for treatment. "Come with me, my brethren," Oyugi begged the old men. "Help me tell Owila that he should leave my house before worse comes upon us."

The old men left their drinks under the tree and hurried to Owila's house. But when they got there, they found Owila standing with his belongings in the yard. Ambajo's wailing for her dying children had driven him out of the house. Owila told his people gravely, "Let me return to Agok, that is where I belong."

Owila and Ogalo took their luggage and followed the little path that wound its way among the coconut trees to the railway station. His relatives walked a little distance behind him. Only a few days ago, they told Owila that his problems were theirs because he was related to them by blood. Now they said nothing. He moved gingerly to the ticket booth. When he had bought their single tickets, they went aboard the train and squeezed themselves in the corner facing the crowd.

Owila felt tired, confused and unwanted. Only the jolt when the train moved away made his heart beat faster, and perspiration ran from his head and down his neck. His relatives started waving, but he was not fully aware of them. He leaned on the window for a long time till nothing more could be seen of the station and his clansmen. And the earth and all life that lived on it speeded away mightily in the opposite direction as if terrified by the *paka-paka-paka-paka* sound of the engine of fire.

At Kisumu station, Owila handed out the luggage to his cousin on the platform. He looked suspiciously at the *kikapu* containing the paraphernalia of his treatment and pushed it right into the corner of the train. If the spirits wanted it, they would find it there.

Then he hurried away from the station with his cousin.

The Rain Came

The chief was still far from the gate when his daughter Oganda saw him. She ran to meet him. Breathlessly she asked her father, "What is the news, great Chief? Everyone in the village is anxiously waiting to hear when it will rain." Labong'o held out his hands for his daughter but he did not say a word. Puzzled by her father's cold attitude Oganda ran back to the village to warn the others that the chief was back.

The atmosphere in the village was tense and confused. Everyone moved aimlessly and fussed in the yard without actually doing any work. A young woman whispered to her co-wife, "If they have not solved this rain business today, the chief will crack." They had watched him getting thinner and thinner as the people kept on pestering him. "Our cattle lie dying in the fields," they reported. "Soon it will be our children and then ourselves. Tell us what to do to save our lives, oh great Chief." So the chief had daily prayed to the Almighty, through the ancestors, to deliver them from their distress.

Instead of calling the family together and giving them the news immediately, Labong'o went to his own hut, a sign that he was not to be disturbed. Having replaced the shutter, he sat in the dimly-lit hut to contemplate.

It was no longer a question of being the chief of hunger-stricken people that weighed Labong'o's heart. It was the life of his only daughter that was at stake. At the time when Oganda came to meet him, he saw the glittering chain shining around her waist. The prophecy was complete. "It is Oganda, Oganda, my only daughter, who must die so young." Labong'o burst into tears before finishing the sentence. The chief must not weep. Society had declared him the bravest of men. But Labong'o did not care any more. He assumed the position of a simple father and wept bitterly. He loved his people, the Luo, but what were the Luo for him without Oganda? Her life had brought a new life into Labong'o's world and he ruled better than he could remember. How would the spirit of the village survive his beautiful daughter? "There are so many homes and so many parents who have daughters. Why choose this one? She is all

I have." Labong'o spoke as if the ancestors were there in the hut and he could see them face to face. Perhaps they were there, warning him to remember his promise on the day he was enthroned when he said aloud, before the elders, "I will lay down life, if necessary, and the life of my household, to save this tribe from the hand's of the enemy."

"Deny! Deny!" he could hear the voice of his fathers mocking him.

When Labong'o was consecrated chief he was only a young man. Unlike his father, he ruled for many years with only one wife. But people rebuked him because his only wife did not bear him a daughter. He married a second, a third, and a fourth wife. But they all gave birth to male children. When Labong'o married a fifth wife, she bore him a daughter. They called her Oganda, meaning "beans", because her skin was very fair. Out of Labong'o's twenty children, Oganda was the only girl. Though she was the chief's favourite, her mother's co-wives swallowed their jealous feelings and showered her with love. After all, they said, Oganda was a female child whose days in the royal family were numbered. She would soon marry at a tender age and leave the enviable position to someone else.

Never in his life had he been faced with such an impossible decision. Refusing to yield to the rainmaker's request would mean sacrificing the whole tribe, putting the interests of the individual above those of the society. More than that it would mean disobeying the ancestors, and most probably wiping the Luo people from the surface of the earth. On the other hand, to let Oganda die as a ransom for the people would permanently cripple Labong'o spiritually. He knew he would never be the same chief again.

The words of Ndithi, the medicine man, still echoed in his ears. "Podho, the ancestor of the Luo, appeared to me in a dream last night, and he asked me to speak to the chief and the people," Ndithi had said to the gathering of tribesmen. "A young woman who has not known a man must die so that the country may have rain. While Podho was still talking to me, I saw a young woman standing at the lakeside, her hands raised, above her head. Her skin was as fair as the skin of young deer in the wilderness. Her tall slender figure stood like a lonely reed at the river bank. Her sleepy eyes wore a sad look like that of a bereaved mother. She wore a gold ring on her left ear, and a glittering brass chain around her waist. As I still marvelled at the beauty of this young woman, Podho told me, "Out of all the women in this land, we have chosen this one. Let her offer herself a sacrifice to the lake monster. And on that day, the rain will come down in torrents. Let everyone stay at home on that day, lest he be carried away by the floods!"

Outside there was a strange stillness, except for the thirsty birds that sang lazily on the dying trees. The blinding midday heat had forced the people to retire to their huts. Not far away from the chief's hut, two guards were snoring away quietly. Labong'o removed his crown and the large eagle-head that hung loosely on his shoulders. He left the hut, and instead of asking Nyabog'o the messenger to beat the drum he went straight and beat it himself. In no time the whole household had assembled under the *siala* tree where he usually addressed them. He told Oganda to wait a while in her grandmother's hut.

When Labong'o stood to address his household, his voice was hoarse and the tears choked him. He started to speak, but words refused to leave his lips. His wives and sons knew there was great danger. Perhaps their enemies had declared war on them. Labong'o's eyes were red, and they could see he had been weeping. At last he told them. "One whom we love and treasure must be taken away from us. Oganda is to die." Labong'o's voice was so faint that he could not hear it himself. But he continued, "The ancestors have chosen her to be offered as a sacrifice to the lake monster in order that we may have rain!"

They were completely stunned. As a confused murmur broke out, Oganda's mother fainted and was carried off to her own hut. But the other people rejoiced. They danced around singing and chanting. "Oganda is the lucky one to die for the people. If it is to save the people, let Oganda go."

In her grandmother's hut Oganda wondered what the whole family were discussing about her that she could not hear. Her grandmother's hut was well away from the chief's court and, much as she strained her ears, she could not hear what they were saying. "It must be marriage," she concluded. It was an accepted custom for the family to discuss their daughter's future marriage behind her back. A faint smile played on Oganda's lips as she thought of the several young men who swallowed saliva at the mere mention of her name.

There was Kech, the son of a neighbouring clan elder. Kech was very handsome. He had sweet, meek eyes and a roaring laughter. He would make a wonderful father, Oganda thought. But they would not be a good match. Kech was a bit too short to be her husband. It would humiliate her to have to look down at Kech each time she spoke to him. Then she thought of Dimo, the tall young man who had already distinguished himself as a brave warrior, and an outstanding wrestler. Dimo adored Oganda, but Oganda thought he would make a cruel husband, always quarrelling and ready to fight. No, she did not like him. Oganda fingered the glittering chain on her waist as she thought of Osinda. A long time ago when she was quite young Osinda had given her that chain, and instead of wearing it around her neck several times, she wore it round her waist where it could stay permanently. She heard her heart pounding so loudly as she thought of him. She whispered, "Let it be you they are discussing, Osinda the lovely one. Come now and take me away ..."

The lean figure in the doorway startled Oganda who was rapt in thought about the man she loved. "You have frightened me, Grandma," said Oganda laughing. "Tell me, is it my marriage you were discussing? You can take it from me that I won't marry any of them." A smile played on her lips again. She was coaxing the old lady to tell her quickly, to tell her they were pleased with Osinda.

In the open space outside, the excited relatives were dancing and singing. They were coming to the hut now, each carrying a gift to put at Oganda's feet. As their singing got nearer Oganda was able to hear what they were saying: "If it is to save the people, if it is to give us rain, let Oganda go. Let Oganda die for her people, and for her ancestors!" Was she mad to think that they were singing about her? How could she die? She found the lean figure of her grandmother barring the door. She could not get out. The look on her grandmother's face warned her that there was danger around the corner. "Grandma, it is not marriage then?" Oganda asked urgently. She suddenly felt panicky like a mouse cornered by a hungry cat. Forgetting that there was only one door in the hut Oganda fought desperately to find another exit. She must fight for her life. But there was none.

She closed her eyes, leapt like a wild tiger through the door, knocking her grandmother flat to the ground. There outside, in mourning garments, Labong'o stood motionless, his hands folded at the back. He held his daughter's hand and led her away from the excited crowd to the little red-painted hut where her mother was resting. Here he broke the news officially to his daughter.

For a long time the three souls who loved one another dearly sat in darkness. It was no good speaking. And even if they tried, the words could not have come out – in the past they had been like three cooking stones, sharing their burdens. Taking Oganda away from them would leave two useless stones which would not hold a cooking pot.

News that the beautiful daughter of the chief was to be sacrificed to give the people rain spread across the country like wind. At sunset the chief's village was full of relatives and friends who had come to congratulate Oganda. Many more were on their way coming, carrying their gifts. They would dance till morning to keep her company. And in the morning they would prepare her a big farewell feast. All these relatives thought it a great honour to be selected by the spirits to die, in order that the society may live. "Oganda's name will always remain a living name among us," they boasted.

But was it maternal love that prevented Minya from rejoicing with the other women? Was it the memory of the agony and pain of childbirth that made her feel so sorrowful? Or was it the deep warmth and understanding that passes between a suckling babe and her mother that made Oganda part of her life, her flesh? Of course it was an honour, a great honour, for her daughter to be chosen to die for the country. But what could she gain once her only daughter was blown away by the wind? There were so many other women in the land, why choose her daughter, her only child! Had human life any meaning at all – other women had houses full of children while she, Minya, had to lose her only child!

In the cloudless sky the moon shone brightly, and the numerous stars glittered with a bewitching beauty. The dancers of all age groups assembled to dance before Oganda, who sat close to her mother, sobbing quietly. All these years she had been with her people she thought she understood them. But now she discovered that she was a stranger among them. If they loved her as they had always professed why were they not making any attempt to save her? Did her people really understand what it felt like to die young? Unable to restrain her emotions any longer, she sobbed loudly as her age group got up to dance. They were young and beautiful, and very soon they would marry and have their own children. They would have husbands to love, and little huts for themselves. They would have reached maturity. Oganda touched the chain around her waist as she thought of Osinda. She wished Osinda was there too, among her friends. "Perhaps he is ill," she thought gravely. The chain comforted Oganda – she would die with it around her waist and wear it in the underground world.

In the morning a big feast was prepared for Oganda. The women prepared many different tasty dishes so that she could pick and choose. "People don't eat after death," they said. Delicious though the food looked, Oganda touched none of it. Let the happy people eat. She contented herself with sips of water from a little calabash.

The time for her departure was drawing near, and each minute was precious. It was a day's journey to the lake. She was to walk all night passing through the great forest. But nothing could touch her, not even the denizens of the forest. She was already anointed with sacred oil. From the time Oganda received the sad news she had expected Osinda to appear any moment. But he was not there. A relative told her that Osinda was away on a private visit. Oganda realised that she would never see her beloved again.

In the afternoon the whole village stood at the gate to say goodbye and to see her for the last time. Her mother wept on her neck for a long time. The great chief in a mourning skin came to the gate bare-footed, and mingled with the people – a simple father in grief. He took off his wrist bracelet and put it on his daughter's wrist saying, "You will always live among us. The spirit of our forefathers is with you!"

Tongue-tied and unbelieving Oganda stood there before the people. She had nothing to say. She looked at her home once more. She could hear her heart beating so painfully within her. All her childhood plans were coming to an end. She felt like a flower nipped in the bud never to enjoy the morning dew again. She looked at her weeping mother, and whispered, "Whenever you want to see me, always look at the sunset. I will be there."

Oganda turned southwards to start her trek to the lake. Her parents, relatives, friends and admirers stood at the gate and watched her go.

Her beautiful slender figure grew smaller and smaller till she mingled with the thin dry trees in the forest. As Oganda walked the lonely path that wound its way in the wilderness, she sang a song, and her own voice kept her company.

> *"The ancestors have said Oganda must die,*
> *The daughter of the chief must be sacrificed,*
> *When the lake monster feeds on my flesh,*
> *The people will have rain.*
> *Yes, the rain will come down in torrents.*
> *And, the floods will wash away the sandy beaches,*
> *When the daughter of the chief dies in the lake.*
> *My age group has consented*
> *My parents have consented*
> *So have my friends and relatives.*
> *Let Oganda die to give us rain.*
> *My age group are young and ripe,*
> *Ripe for womanhood and motherhood,*
> *But Oganda must die young,*
> *Oganda must sleep with the ancestors.*
> *Yes, rain will come down in torrents."*

The red rays of the setting sun embraced Oganda, and she looked like a burning candle in the wilderness.

The people who came to hear her sad song were touched by her beauty. But they all said the same thing: "If it is to save the people, if it is to give us rain, then be not afraid. Your name will forever live among us."

At midnight Oganda was tired and weary. She could walk no more. She sat under a big tree and having sipped water from her calabash, she rested her head on the tree trunk and slept.

When Oganda woke up in the morning the sun was high in the sky. After walking for many hours, she reached the *tong'*, a strip of land that separated the inhabited part of the country from the sacred place *(kar lamo)*. No layman could enter this place and come out alive – only those who had direct contact with the spirits and the Almighty were allowed to enter this holy of holies. But Oganda had to pass through this sacred land on her way to the lake, which she had to reach at sunset.

A large crowd gathered to see her for the last time. Her voice was now hoarse and painful, but there was no need to worry any more. Soon she would not have to sing. The crowd looked at Oganda sympathetically, mumbling words she could not hear. But none of them pleaded for life. As Oganda opened the gate, a child, a young child, broke loose from the crowd, and ran towards her. The child took a small earring from her sweaty hands and gave it to Oganda saying, "When you reach the world of the dead, give this earring to my sister. She died last week. She forgot this ring." Oganda, taken aback by the strange request, took the little ring, and handed her precious water and food to the child. She did not need them now. Oganda did not know whether to laugh or cry. She had heard mourners sending their love to their sweethearts, long dead, but this idea of sending gifts was new to her.

Oganda held her breath as she crossed the barrier to enter the sacred land. She looked appealingly at the crowd, but there was no response. Their minds were too pre–occupied with their own survival. Rain was the precious medicine they were longing for, and the sooner Oganda could get to her destination the better.

A strange feeling possessed Oganda as she picked her way in the sacred land. There were strange noises that often startled her, and her first reaction was to take to her heels. But she remembered that she had to fulfil the wish of her people. She was exhausted, but the path was still winding. Then suddenly the path ended on sandy land. The water had retreated miles away from the shore, leaving a wide stretch of sand. Beyond this was the vast expanse of water.

Oganda felt afraid. She wanted to picture the size and shape of the monster, but fear would not let her. The society did not talk about it, nor did the crying children who were silenced by the mention of its name. The sun was still up, but it was no longer hot. For a long time Oganda walked ankle-deep in the sand. She was exhausted and longed desperately for the calabash of water. As she moved on, she had a strange feeling that something was following her. Was it the monster? Her hair stood erect, and a cold paralysing feeling ran along her spine. She looked behind, sideways and in front, but there was nothing, except a cloud of dust.

Oganda pulled up and hurried but the feeling did not leave her, and her whole body became saturated with perspiration.

The sun was going down fast and the lake shore seemed to move along with it. Oganda started to run. She must be at the lake before sunset. As she ran she heard a noise coming from behind. She looked back sharply, and something resembling a moving bush was frantically running after her. It was about to catch up with her.

Oganda ran with all her strength. She was now determined to throw herself into the water even before sunset. She did not look back, but the creature was upon her. She made an effort to cry out, as in a nightmare, but she could not hear her own voice. The creature caught up with Oganda. In the utter confusion, as Oganda came face to face with the unidentified creature, a strong hand grabbed her. But she fell flat on the sand and fainted.

When the lake breeze brought her back to consciousness, a man was bending over her. "................!" Oganda opened her mouth to speak, but she had lost her voice. She swallowed a mouthful of water poured into her mouth by the stranger.

"Osinda, Osinda! Please let me die. Let me run, the sun is going down. Let me die, let them have rain." Osinda fondled the glittering chain around Oganda's waist and wiped the tears from her face.

"We must escape quickly to the unknown land," Osinda said urgently. "We must run away from the wrath of the ancestors and the retaliation of the monster."

"But the curse is upon me, Osinda, I am no good to you any more. And moreover the eyes of the ancestors will follow us everywhere and bad luck will befall us. Nor can we escape from the monster."

Oganda broke loose, afraid to escape, but Osinda grabbed her hands again.

"Listen to me, Oganda! Listen! Here are two coats!" He then covered the whole of Oganda's body, except her eyes with a leafy attire made from the twigs of *bwombwe*. "These will protect us from the eyes of the ancestors and the wrath of the monster. Now let us run out of here." He held Oganda's hand and they ran from the sacred land, avoiding the path that Oganda had followed.

The bush was thick, and the long grass entangled their feet as they ran. Halfway through the sacred land they stopped and looked back. The sun was almost touching the surface of the water. They were frightened. They continued to run, now faster, to avoid the sinking sun.

"Have faith Oganda, that thing will not reach us."

When they reached the barrier and looked behind them trembling, only a tip of the sun could be seen above the water's surface.

"It is gone! It is gone!" Oganda wept, hiding her face in her hands.

"Weep not, daughter of the chief. Let us run, let us escape."

There was a bright flash of lightning. They looked up, frightened. Above them black furious clouds started to gather. They began to run. Then the thunder roared, and the rain came down in torrents.

Night Sister

The clock on the wall struck 11.30 am. A sharp pain developed over my stomach becoming really painful around my navel. I bit my teeth and clenched the edge of the mantelpiece. The pain became excruciating for about three seconds. Then slowly, too slowly, it disappeared leaving me numb. It was an awkward hour to bother anyone. People were rushing to finish off last minute jobs before closing for lunch. Instead of going to the phone, I went to the book shelf and pulled out Dr Valley's book – *Childbirth Without Pain*. I thumbed through it and found what I was looking for. "There we are," I said aloud. The headlines stared at me – SIGNS THAT LABOUR HAVE STARTED. I read them a couple of times as I had done before. In fact, I had read the words over and over again during the first months and I knew them by heart. Yet now I wanted to consult the book once more just to be double sure.

I moved about the house restlessly. Our helper was downstairs handling the washing. I did not want him to notice any change in me. The doctor had told me that there was no need to rush to hospital as soon as some pain started. There were things like false labour pains. Another painful contraction came. I was in the middle of the kitchen facing the main door, and I could not move. I clutched the door panting like a thirsty dog. At that very moment Sango came in with a basin in one hand and a peg holder in the other. I was obstructing his way to the kitchen. I wanted to move, to hide my feelings and pretend I just had a cramp as I had done so many times in the past, but I could not. We each held our ground. When what seemed like two full minutes had slowly passed by and the pain had gone, I stood erect and walked towards the bedroom without saying anything.

"Are you all right, madam?" Sango, asked nervously. His question irritated me, and I did not answer. "Why can't he go on with his work and leave me alone," I groaned. I knew he meant well but the fact that he had seen me at that particular time annoyed me.

I went into the bathroom and started running the water. I wanted to have a bath, or did I? I had had one when I got up late in the morning. I had not been anywhere. I turned off the water and went to the bedroom. Everything there stared at me and my heart was beating slightly faster than usual, and the corners of my eyes were stinging with tears.

"Why are you being childish and foolish?" I said aloud. "You may have started true labour. What is wrong about that to make you behave like a child." I got on my knees to pray. The words were few and disjointed, but I rumbled on.

I dragged my heavy body from the floor and as I stood up, I came face to face with my husband, standing on the doorway looking at me unbelievingly.

"You startled me," I said angrily. "Why do you sneak in like that? I have told you so many times that I get easily frightened nowadays." And tears bubbled from my eyes. He realised I was serious.

"But, my dear, I did not mean to startle you. I opened the door and walked in the usual way. Then I heard you praying, so I waited."

He must have heard what I was praying about, I thought bitterly. So I changed the subject quickly.

"How come you are home so early?" Suddenly I was grateful for his presence.

"We closed early today to enable staff to attend the funeral of poor Mr Robinson who died last night." His words trailed away in the air and I did not catch the last word, I made as if to grip his shoulders but I changed my mind. I leaned back on the bed and gripped the wood tightly. Ochieng threw his arm around me, and the tightness of my abdomen frightened him.

"Can I call the ambulance?"

He was all in a panic. When the pain subsided and I stood facing him, he asked me urgently, "What do we do?"

"We go and have lunch," I laughed.

"Don't be funny," he said seriously. "We must do something now about you."

"I am not being funny. The immediate thing I must do is to eat something. It may be a long wait, so I need enough strength."

My husband stared at me blankly.

"All right, just what you say."

We ate hurriedly. Ochieng had no appetite and I was racing against time. By 1.00 pm. the pains were so regular that I could not even hide them from Sango, who constantly peered at me through the opening between the kitchen and the dining room.

We arrived at Watukufu Hospital at 1.45 pm. A man standing at the gate showed us the way to the admission department. We walked and walked through a very long corridor that seemed to have no end. Four times I rested on Ochieng's shoulders with frantic pains.

"Aren't we there yet?" I moaned, refusing to move an inch. A man in a brown uniform walked towards us.

"*Wapi Admission?*" Ochieng asked urgently.

"*Pa - a -le upande wa kulia.*" (There on the right.)

I stood and looked – the corridor stretched beyond my eyes and I could not see any turning. I propelled myself along stopping now and again when I had a pain. At long last we reached the Admission Room abruptly on the right. I sank on the nearest bench – exhausted.

"New patient?" the grey-haired woman on the counter asked.

"Yes," my husband replied sulkily. "What a long way for patients to walk. Wouldn't it have been more sensible to have the Admission Room near the entrance of the hospital?"

"That is the work of the architect," the woman replied with little concern. "I am just a receptionist, and I have not been in this place for long. And what is the name of the patient?"

"Hana Ochieng."

"I take it you are the husband?"

Ochieng nodded.

"Mrs Ochieng, do you need a wheel chair or can you walk?" The woman now addressed me.

"How far is the walk?" I asked miserably.

"Past the entrance where you came."

"All that way back," I exclaimed.

"Yes, I am afraid so."

"I will walk," I said firmly.

"Are you sure?" the woman asked me again.

But I did not reply. Instead I stood up, ready to move. A porter in brown uniform led the way. After walking what looked like a good quarter of a mile to me, we reached the St. Mary's Ward, in the modern wing of the hospital.

The pains were now more regular and I was really worried. A plump looking European nurse took us to the waiting room. Her kind attitude made me relax a little. Then she took me in a single room which we wanted. The charges were 120/- a day, she told my husband who accepted this without question. He was asked to wait in the waiting room while the nurse examined me. While she bent over me I read the name plate pinned on her chest: "Sister Wood". When she had finished she smiled at me. "You are doing well. Part of the baby's head has gone down and your contractions are strong, but as it is the first baby it may take time, at least 8 to 10 hours before we see the baby. So try to relax and be patient.

But don't hesitate to ring the bell to call us if you need anything. We are quite close all the time. All right, dear?"

"Thank you, Sister," I murmured.

"Nurse will give you a small enema – I'm sure you know what that means?"

"Yes," I replied, "and I hate enemas."

"It's not very comfortable, I know, but at this time, I am sure you can endure anything to hasten the coming of your baby." She was right. She left me and went to get some details from Ochieng.

I had always been afraid of hospitals and the impatience of overworked nurses. Many patients spoke ill of the nurses. Many expecting mothers were scared of the hospitals, and I had heard some terrible stories. But Sister Wood's words comforted me. Ten hours sounded a long time, but her angelic face would help me and encourage me. It would be wonderful to go out of the hospital and to tell all my friends that I did the right thing to come to Watukufu Hospital and that the nurses were wonderful. At that moment I had a very strong contraction, but I no longer gripped the bed. I was now more relaxed.

Nurse Wairimu who attended me was gentle and she had a strikingly beautiful face which qualified her to be a filmstar. I told her so and she blushed. Ochieng came to see me briefly but soon left on the Sister's orders.

At 3.00 pm the Sister gave me an injection. It made me dizzy and light in the head. The contractions came and went but I was sleepy and exhausted.

"Listen Mrs Ochieng," the Sister told me. "This injection will make you very drowsy. Don't get out of bed now. If you need anything, just press the bell, one of us will come to you."

"Thank you, Sister," I said quietly, and within a few minutes I fell asleep. The pains became more regular and strong but I slept quite deeply in between. Ochieng returned at 5.00 pm and sat with me for a while but I was not fully aware of his presence. He had never seen a woman in labour. He later told me that he was sick in his stomach as he heard my groans when the pain came.

At about 8.00 pm I was wide awake and the pains were wild. I closed my eyes but sleep had disappeared. Something told me that I must not cry. Thousands of women had done this before. In the village where I was brought up, several women gave birth without anybody even knowing about it. People were only surprised to see the baby. There was no one else but the village midwife – no modern medicines to relieve the pain and make them sleepy. Women who cried during childbirth in the village were scorned by their fellows.

Nurse Wairimu helped me wash, and gave me some pudding and sweetened milk.

"I am going off duty now." She pressed my hand.

"And the Sister too?" I cried.

"Yes," she said. "All of us. Good luck and give us a surprise when we come in the morning. Bye!" She pressed my hand again, and closed the door behind her without looking back.

A little bitterness hushed through my heart – none of my friends had told me that having a baby was so tedious and painful. Only four months ago, Sango's wife had walked home with a baby from Pumwani Maternity Hospital. She was in pain the whole day without complaining or even telling her husband. Later that day when they asked Ochieng to take them to hospital, she nearly delivered in the car. When I asked her why she did not tell anybody that she was in labour, she replied with a laugh,

"Hm, there was no need to alarm people. I know I had to do it, and it is embarrassing for the whole world to know that you are in labour!"

Nyaboro never went to school. She was partially a Catholic, but this did not interfere with her strong beliefs. One day, when she returned from Nyanza and found a lot of new nappies rinsed and hung on the line, she asked Sango urgently. "Has she had the baby. I thought her baby was not coming for a few months." Sango told her that the baby had not come, but I had bought so many things for my already unborn baby including a bath and a cot, and a feeding bottle.

"Hm!" she said with a dry laugh. "These educated people! They go out of their way to call bad luck. How does she know that she is carrying a baby, or that the baby will be born alive?"

They were speaking near the kitchen window on the yard and her words caused a pang of pain in my heart.

Contractions came and went, but a stabbing backache now remained with me all the time. At the thought of Nyaboro's words, a kind of naive fear bothered me. Was the baby going to come out alive?

The door opened with a bang and startled me. A stout tall sister walked in.

"How are we doing in here?" and before I could answer she had stripped the bed clothes from my neck right down below my waist. " Lie on your back, please."

I obeyed. She examined me roughly and her very cold hands made me clench the bedsheets.

"Relax, relax," she shouted.

"Well, your hands are so cold," I protested. I realised that I did not like her attitude.

"Well, it is freezing outside," she told me bluntly. "You are lucky to be in a cosy warm bed."

"Nurse Gertrude!" she called.

"Yes, Sister," someone replied.

"Bring me the examination tray right away."

"Yes, Sister." I heard the nurse hurry away. Meanwhile, I had a very strong pain and my tears ran freely – partly because of the pain and partly because I did not like the Night Sister.

She finished examining me and washed out at the wash basin close to my bed. Then she faced me.

"You are not anywhere near having the baby. So there is no need for shedding tears. I will give you another injection. Try to relax and sleep. The baby will come tomorrow."

"But the Sister who examined me at 7.30 pm told me the baby would come tonight." Tears choked me and a big lump blocked my throat causing pain.

"I don't care what the other Sister told you. Just listen to what I am telling you. You are not anywhere near. You tense up yourself crying instead of relaxing. That is what will delay the baby. Turn on your side." I obeyed, then she drew up the bed clothes and flopped them on my weary body, tucking each side tight. She took the tray, opened the door and let it close with a bang. I disentangled my right arm and brought it above the blanket. "Where is that motherly African Nurse who brought the tray in and left without talking to me?" I cried aloud.

I wanted to ring the bell, but decided against it. Something told me that Sister Smith would come again.

I was very scared by her. Anger mixed with pain and anxiety weighed my heart. I gripped the bed clothes and wept. The confidence that I had built up on my arrival to the hospital was now crumbling down. I had wanted to go to a Catholic hospital where I was told the nuns cared for the sick tenderly, but it was very far away from our house and we decided against it. Now I wished I had had a baby during the day while Sister Wood was on duty.

Deep sleep was pulling at my body again, almost taking me away by force. I struggled and glanced at my watch. It was 2 am. I was tired and depressed, and grateful to be sleepy. I woke up with a start from a dream. I had been dreaming that the sun was up, and that Ochieng was sitting near me asking for the baby. I jumped and sat up but I felt so drowsy and crumpled back on the bed. A big contraction came, and another and another. I felt desperately that I wanted to pass urine. I fumbled for the bell and pressed it. It rang, I heard it. Meanwhile, I held my buttocks tight to keep the urine back. I listened but nobody was coming. Thinking that perhaps nobody had heard me I pressed the bell again. Presently the door opened.

"What is the matter now?"

The very person I did not want to see stood at the door. She put on the lights full blast and I could not see.

"I want to pass urine please."

"That is all right," her voice was clearly saying. "Who is stopping you? Just hop down and go to the toilet."

I thought I had not heard what she said, and the words just slipped out of my mouth. "I beg your pardon?"

"Just hop-down-and-go-to-the-toilet," She said the words slowly and distinctly to be quite sure that I understood her and she left me, this time leaving the door open.

My first reaction was to pass urine in bed but I got out of it quickly. It was a very long time since I had wet my bedding. I was a very young girl then before I went to school. I would not do it now. I hopped out of bed, and my feet felt as light as a feather. I moved a few steps towards the door. Another strong contraction came, pushing the urine out and in spite of my effort I felt streaks of water running down my legs. I made an effort to hurry and get to the toilet but somehow, my feet did not touch the floor. I was very light in the head, and a ghostly thought told me that I would fall down and crack my head on the floor and kill my unborn child. I hastened my steps. Where was the toilet? Or had I passed it? Then I saw it. The door was open. One desperate step and I flopped on the toilet pan exhausted. I heard a few drops of urine trickling in the pan. Then a terrific pain came and I felt the baby was coming while I was sitting on the toilet pan. I made a desperate effort to get up, but the pain continued and I remained fixed on the pan. As soon as the pain subsided I struggled to my room. My mind was blank, and I tried to avoid the thought that the baby may drop on the floor and die. I reached my room and clambered on my bed, panting. Almost immediately, a flood of water ran from me making a big pool round my buttocks. I pressed the bell. Presently, the motherly looking nurse came, beaming with sympathy. I threw my hands round her, caressing her starched apron. I did not even know what I was doing.

"Where have you been? That groggy 'Mubeberu' of a Sister nearly killed me. Don't leave me now." I had never used the word 'Mubeberu' before, nor was I political. The word just slipped out.

"I think something has happened here," I showed her. She opened the blanket and found a big pool.

"Don't worry, dear," she told me. "I think the bag of water is ruptured. The baby will soon be here. Let me call the Sister." My heart sank. Within minutes the sister was in my room. "Did you go to the toilet as I told you?" she asked quickly.

"I did," I said bitterly. "I have just got back."

"Then you came to pass the rest of the urine in the bed," she snapped.

"Don't be ridiculous, Sister" I was annoyed.

"I am an adult. I cannot pass urine in bed. Why don't you cheek first before making up your mind that it is urine?"

She bent and looked at the bedding.

"Yes, looks like urine," she said with finality. Then while she stood there arguing I had a big contraction, more water rushed out of me splashing over her white apron and the floor. A feeling of triumph comforted me. God was not a fool. The nurse looked at me, then at the Sister. "Oh, then she has ruptured membranes, nurse." She sounded so disappointed.

"Bring clean sheets, I will change, her."

Nurse left the room. Then the telephone rang and the Sister also left to my great relief. Nurse returned immediately and changed the bed clothes, swiftly but gently. I helped whenever I could between the pains. Then she asked me to lie on my back.

"Goodness," she gasped. "Did you really pass urine? And why did you go out of bed," she asked me urgently.

"Sister told me to. I passed very little urine."

"You should not walk that long way all alone because of those injections. Moreover you have a very full bladder. See." She put my hand over the swelling then I understood. The swelling had been there for some time. With a contraction, my tummy divided distinctly into big lumps. Knowing nothing, I had assumed that perhaps it was the baby's head. Nurse went and told the Sister that I had a very full bladder.

"She has just passed urine," I heard the Sister say.

"The bladder is dangerously full," the nurse urged.

"You know nothing," the Sister shouted at her. "You go and attend to Mrs Wilson who is crying next door."

The telephone rang again and the Sister went to the office. Nurse came to me.

"Don't be afraid. I will attend to that patient who is crying and then I will come to you."

I grabbed her hands.

After what seemed like a long nightmare. I felt sure the baby was coming. I could not hold it back. I rang the bell frantically. Nurse Gertrude came running.

"The baby is coming," I gasped, as soon as she put her head through the door. She looked. She ran back, obviously to tell Sister Smith.

I heard a shrill voice, "Nonsense – I have just examined her and she is nowhere near. Tell her to relax and sleep, that woman is really getting on my nerves."

"No, Sister, you must come and see for yourself. The baby is coming."

"Stop arguing with me, Nurse. Get on with your work with that new patient in the waiting room."

"Sister, if you don't come, I will deliver her. I have had a baby. I know what that woman is going through." She left the Sister standing there. I pressed the bell once and then a second time and I no longer heard their voices. I was alone in the room and I panicked. Nurse Gertrude came in first. The Sister ran after her. They flung the bed clothes from me. I had terrible pains and my tummy had divided into two heaps.

Without a word the Sister ran for the trolley herself. Within minutes I was on the hard ward bed. The sister stripped me naked. My teeth chattered but I persevered. She rinsed her hands and put a small rubber in to get the urine out. Within a minute one dish was full and then a second one. She could not believe her eyes. Yet more urine was still coming out. Suddenly the pain that was cutting my lower tummy ceased.

The clock on the wall ...

Sister had disappeared through another door. Nurse Gertrude clasped my hands. Pains now came without stopping. The Sister was back in the room.

"Don't push, don't push," she shouted. But I was not listening. I had waited long enough, and however hard I tried to tighten my muscles, I could not hold the baby back. She moved closer to my bed and grabbed my hands.

"Don't push, you hear me. Open your mouth and breathe in and out." But I was wild with confusion and pain. The baby was ready to come out. Sister was telling me not to push. What was wrong, or did she want my baby to die. It had happened to some mothers, it could happen to me.

"Nurse, Nurse." I broke loose from the Sister and grabbed her hands. She was an African like me. What was the game the Sister was playing?

"Why must I not push." I demanded. "My baby will die, please tell me please."

"We are waiting for the doctor," Nurse whispered to me tearfully.

"Why could you not call him earlier, Nurse? Why could you not call him earlier – all this time I have been struggling and pleading – all this ..."

The labour ward door opened and a man in white overalls walked in. I knew him. He was the man I had seen week after week for over eight months. Somehow the light of a saviour shone brightly on his face and a naive kind of peace replaced the panic that had tortured my heart throughout the night.

"Now push, Mrs Ochieng," Sister Smith told me pleasantly. She was a real hypocrite, and could act good when it suited her. The doctor washed quickly and was standing by me encouraging me. Within minutes my baby was born. The doctor announced that I had a daughter.

"We will call her Nyangisa," I said without thinking.

"What does that mean," the doctor asked me.

"It means a lot to me," I said slowly. "It is the name of my husband's mother who died when my husband was a boy. We wanted so much to have a daughter first."

The doctor pressed my hand in an understanding manner. Nurse Gertrude looked at me in wonder. Sister Smith was nowhere to be seen. When the stitches had been put in and I was holding our daughter in my arms, I was at peace with the world. I closed my eyes and prayed silently.

"One who went away has
come back to live with us.
Ochieng will be so pleased."

Elizabeth

It had just struck 8 o'clock when Elizabeth entered her new office. Immediately the telephone rang, and she picked it up nervously.

"Hallo, 21201."

"Hallo there, is that Mr Jimbo's secretary?"

"Speaking, can I help you?" Elizabeth tugged the telephone under her chin and drew a pad and a pencil from the drawer.

"Oh yes, may I speak to Mr Jimbo, please."

"Sorry, he has not come yet; he does not come till 8.30 am. Could you kindly ring again, please?"

"Right I will do that."

"Hallo – hallo ..." but Elizabeth heard the click on the other side and then the usual buzzing sound. She replaced the receiver with a bang, annoyed that she had not got the caller's name.

The door leading to Mr Jimbo's office stood open. The spacious office, with a huge mahogany desk and a deep green carpet covering the floor, was neatly arranged. There were no curtains on the windows; instead, light Venetian blinds were drawn up on the large windows facing the main road, suggesting that the sun entered the offices in the afternoon. Everything was neatly arranged on the table and a photograph of a very attractive woman holding two little boys stood smartly at one corner, like watchmen guarding the office. Elizabeth scrutinised the photograph and then returned it to its place. She went back to her office and stood at the little window to look at the jammed traffic below. The offices of the Department of Aviation were in Manila House on the 4th floor on Heroes Lane. From there one could see a good part of the city and the stretch of the empty land that extended along the Mombasa Road to the airport.

Elizabeth wondered how long she would stay in the Department of Aviation. She had moved from two offices in a matter of months since she returned from the US where she had taken her secretarial training. She first worked for four months in a big American motor firm as secretary to the Assistant Manager; and when that failed she found employment with the Wholesalers and Distributors Limited, as secretary to the European Manager. After two agonising months, and unable to satisfy the demands of her boss, Elizabeth walked out of her job without giving any notice. Both bosses had given her the impression that she ought to be a cheap girl ready to sell her body for promotion and money. When Elizabeth turned up at the Department of Aviation for interview, the Personnel Officer apologetically but conclusively told her that they could only take her on at £790 per annum, instead of her previous salary of £850.

Footsteps on the stairs alerted Elizabeth. She walked back to her desk and busied herself on the typewriter. Presently, the door opened and Mr Jimbo walked in. Elizabeth got up automatically and opened the door leading to the main office after murmuring, "Good morning." Her new boss eyed Elizabeth from foot to head and then sat heavily on a rocking chair. Elizabeth closed the door gently and continued with her work.

Before long the bell rang, and a green light flickered above the internal line. Elizabeth picked up the receiver.

"Would you come for dictation right away please?"

"Yes, sir, right away." She picked up her shorthand notebook and pencil and entered the main office.

"Sit down, will you."

Elizabeth obeyed. At that moment the private telephone rang, and Mr Jimbo relaxed in the rocking chair and spoke leisurely to the caller. Elizabeth examined her new boss surreptitiously. He was about 40 years or so. About 5' 9, jet black, he had an oily skin, chubby face and boldly brushed black hair. His upper teeth looked too white to be real and his dark gums exaggerated the whiteness. His deep fatherly voice was full of confidence and authority. He did not look the mischievous type nor did he look fierce. But Elizabeth knew that time alone could tell: she would do her best to stay on the job this time, if only to avoid being a rolling stone.

"Right, see you and madam at about 8.00 pm. Bye."

He replaced the receiver and started dictating straight away.

At 11.00 am. Elizabeth had typed a heap of letters and placed them before Mr Jimbo for his signature. He frowned at her "That was quick."

Elizabeth smiled and closed the door behind her. She had been warned about the amount of work in Jimbo's office by the previous secretary, but she was confident she would manage. By 12.15 pm. she had cleared her desk, and she walked out for lunch feeling less nervous than she had been in the morning.

The following Monday a beautiful woman walked into Elizabeth's office to see Mr Jimbo, who was having a meeting with senior members of the department. Elizabeth wondered where she had seen the woman before. She was tall and slim, with a pale chocolate skin and a startling hair style.

"Is he busy?" she asked cautiously.

"Yes, he is having a meeting," Elizabeth told her. "What is your name please? I will tell him on the phone."

"I am his wife," the lady told her with a genuine smile.

"Now I remember where I've seen you! I have seen the beautiful photograph you took with your two sons. Please sit down, Mrs Jimbo. I will mention to him that you are here."

Elizabeth pressed the bell and whispered, "Your wife is here, shall I tell her to wait?"

"No, I will speak to her right away."

The telephone clicked, and before Elizabeth could give the message, Mr Jimbo stood at the door.

"Sorry, Amy dear, would you take the driver, the meeting is still going on. I will give you a ring when I finish."

"Right, will be hearing from you then." She turned to Elizabeth. "I'd better be going."

Amy Jimbo thanked Elizabeth and left with the driver. She looked a contented good wife. Elizabeth believed in a happy marriage – that was her secret dream. Now to see the Jimbos so confident and in love intensified her longing for her lover at Ohio State University in the United States where he was finishing his post graduate studies in engineering. She stared into space for a while, and then returned to her typewriter.

The busy weeks slipped into months, and when Easter came, Elizabeth with two girlfriends took a long weekend to Mombasa where they did nothing but bathe, eat and write the longest love letters they had ever written. For Liz, there was plenty to be thankful for. At last God had answered her prayers: she was working among people who respected her womanhood and capabilities. Mr Jimbo had given her the respect she had longed for and other members of staff had not molested her in any way. Sometimes he had given her much work, and often she worked late in the evenings when all other secretaries had gone home. True, during the past weeks, with plenty of late hours, she had experienced moments of fear. But what had calmed her eventually was Jimbo himself; the fatherly boss. He once told Elizabeth, "I hate to leave you to walk to the hostel alone when it is so late, but I don't believe in giving lifts to young girls. Soon the town would start gossiping and you would get a bad name for nothing. You have a long future in front of you, my child. You should protect your name."

The girls arrived back in the city by night train, ready for work on Tuesday. With only a few days to go before the International Aviation Conference in Nairobi, Mr Jimbo's desk was piled with numerous draft documents for stencilling. And a pile of cards to be sent out for a cocktail party to be held on the eve of the conference still stood untouched. Elizabeth worked late each evening to reduce the pile. Mr Jimbo gave her a spare key so that she could leave the office when she pleased. He also instructed the watchman to be around the building whenever Elizabeth was working late.

That Saturday afternoon was particularly hot. Liz glanced at her watch; it was about 1.30 pm. As she covered her typewriter to dash out for lunch, the door was flung open and there stood Mr Jimbo beaming at the door. "You poor kid – still working! The world is not ending today, my dear."

"Thank you, sir, I have finished now. I will have plenty of time when the conference is over next week – have you forgotten something, sir?"

"No, I thought you might still be working and I came to release you."

"That is kind of you," Elizabeth answered with a smile. It was rare to have bosses who really cared about the amount of work their secretaries did, she thought.

Jimbo walked into his office, and Elizabeth took her handbag and magazines ready to leave.

"All right, sir, I am off now."

"Just a second." He fumbled with some papers and then looked up. "I have more packed lunch here than I really need – here, have a bite."

Elizabeth did not want to share Mr Jimbo's packed lunch – he had not expected to find her in the office anyway and she knew Mr Jirnbo was just being polite.

"Thank you, sir, but I would rather not – my lunch will be waiting at the hostel."

"Go on, don't be shy. I can't eat all these, come in and sit down."

"No, sir, I really must go, I would rather have a proper lunch – I missed breakfast."

"Come on, don't argue, just one."

Out of sheer politeness, Elizabeth went in and sat on a settee. She did not want to appear rude to a man who had treated her with such great respect. Yet she hated his persuasiveness. He handed her a packet, and she picked out an egg sandwich. Then out of the blue, the boss moved over and sat with a big sigh beside Elizabeth on the settee.

"I am impressed with your work, my girl. Since you came, this office looks different. One never really knows what a good and efficient secretary is until one has one." He paused and picked up another sandwich.

"Thank you sir – pleasure is mine – you are an easy person to work for. I was not that good till I came to this establishment." She tried to dodge the rough surface of Jimbo's tweed coat that rubbed against her upper arm.

"I'm glad to hear that. The only thing that worries me is this, my child." He fingered the little diamond ring on Elizabeth's left finger.

"Oh that sir, nothing doing for another two years or so and by that time a lot of changes will have taken place."

She almost told him the truth: that Ochola was coming back in November and they planned to get married on New Year's day but that was still a secret.

"Who is he – I mean this lucky chap, what does he do?

"Still a student," Elizabeth answered nervously.

"He is lucky, a real lucky man to possess you. You are efficient, you are feminine, and you are very beautiful." And his heavy arm went round Elizabeth's slender waist and gripped her tight.

"Oh please, sir, please – stop this – please," and she struggled to her feet.

"Listen to me, Liz – listen," Mr Jimbo spoke sternly.

"I can't hurt you. I like you like my own child, I can't hurt you – honestly. I – I just wanted to tell you that you are so enchanting, and I – I just wanted to feel your body close to mine, but I won't hurt you. I promise."

She felt the hard pounding of his heart. He looked at her warmly, with yearning. Elizabeth pulled herself together and broke loose from Jimbo's grip. The humid air stifled her.

"Please, sir – let me go, I am engaged to get married soon – please, Ochola will not understand, nor will your wife, your children and the people. And think of my job – oh please, let me go," and she sobbed aloud.

"Now you are to behave like a good girl, the people will hear us and think of the scandal. I've told you that I can't hurt you – I care too much to hurt you." He locked the door and put the key in his coat pocket. Beads of perspiration stood on his nose and his forehead, his muscles were as taut as the top of a drum, and his face was wild with excitement.

Elizabeth never suspected that beneath the firm crust of Jimbo's restrained face, a volcano simmered. Physical contact had provoked an eruption. "I just want to feel your breasts, nothing more – then we can go to lunch."

He moved over to her, but she ducked behind the desk and then to the window, and to the door and back to the desk. But Jimbo caught up with her and dragged her to the settee. He searched for Elizabeth's mouth but the girl was too violent and buried her face in her skirt. "Please Liz." He kissed her ears and her neck, then her upper arm, while his big hands reached desperately for the young breasts. His hot breath and the masculine odour that radiated from his body made Elizabeth quite sick. She drew away from him, her face in a grimace of pain.

"No, Liz, you're so lovable," he whispered. "Your lovely skin is smooth and tender like the petals of a flower. No, no, I can't hurt – I can't, I care too much. Just let me feel the warmth of your womanhood. I won't hurt you, Liz. I promise, I do – I do –." Elizabeth fought helplessly beneath this bulky man who had posed as an angel for so many months. And it was like one of those terrible nightmares without an end.

The day was spent. Elizabeth threw blankets off from her body. Her pillow was damp, and the crumpled photograph of her fiancé which she was tightly embracing when she dozed off to sleep had fallen on the floor. She got up slowly and walked to the window facing the city centre. The pain between her legs had worsened and her whole body was aching as it did on the first day when her friend tried to teach her to ride a bicycle. The city looked peaceful except for a few cars moving homewards away from the business area. The tip of Manila Building could just be seen facing Embakasi Airport which it served. Down below in the central park were hundreds of sightseers, mostly Asians — sitting in groups, men and women segregated. Their innocent children ran wildly like bees among flowers. As a child, Elizabeth had felt happy chasing grasshoppers in the open fields below her home opposite the River Nzoia. She and her little cousin had looked forward to the time when they would be adults. They wanted to discuss adult subjects and perform adult duties.

Then she thought of the day when her periods came at the age of eleven, how she ran to her grandmother's hut weeping that she was sick and how her granny comforted her and told her that she was now a woman and must behave like an adult, and stop playing with boys. She remembered how she had looked her in the eye and asked innocently: "What do you mean?"

To which her granny had replied, "When a mature girl plays with boys, it is like a child playing with fire; the child can burn herself and probably burn her parent's house and cause great sadness. In the same way, when a mature girl plays with boys and becomes pregnant outside of wedlock, she destroys herself and eventually destroys the whole family."

Although she did not understand the words of her grandmother, the horror in her face indicated to her that it was a bad thing and she ran back to her mother's house reciting the words – "it is like a child playing with fire; It can cause much sadness."

Elizabeth drew up the curtain to shut out the city and its people from her. She felt out of step with the sophisticated life in towns. She wondered whether she would ever get used to it. A sudden aching longing for her home in the country, the close-knit family life she had shared there, and the security she had felt, gripped her. She took her toilet bag and walked slowly to the washroom. She entered the incinerator room, pulled out her blood-stained nylon pants that Ochola had sent her for Easter and wrapped them lightly in a brown paper bag. She pressed the incinerator open, and dropped the pants in the fire and let it close. She stood there sobbing quietly as the pale smoke reluctantly curled up towards the sky. Jimbo had robbed her of the treasure she had hidden away for so many years. Her whole world had fallen apart, and she felt nothing but bitterness and sorrow at the thought that she had nothing left to offer her man on the wedding day.

Elizabeth left the hostel early Monday morning with a group of friends. But instead of catching the double-decker bus that went to Heroes Street, she took a footpath across the central park towards Stalion Road. She walked briskly, dodging the stream of cars that poured into the city. When she reached the Labour Office at 8.00 am, hundreds of women of all ages had already arrived and were waiting for the doors to be opened. Some gray-haired women sat in a group, talking in low voices. Elizabeth's heart went out for them. Sorrow had eaten away their youth, leaving permanent lines on their foreheads.

As the number swelled, their morose faces reminded Elizabeth of the seekers of the kingdom of God who used to throng her father's church on Sunday, when she was small. But no! She felt that God must have moved to another land where people acted more justly.

A hand resting on Elizabeth's shoulders startled her, and she turned round sharply.

"Liz, what are you doing here? Come into the office." She followed the Labour Officer into the crowded office and sat down.

"Don't tell me you have left that job again!" Elizabeth nodded.

"Why this time Elizabeth, were they being naughty again?" She nodded.

Mrs Kimani, a middle-aged motherly woman had dealt with hundreds of cases similar to Elizabeth's and seeing that Elizabeth did not want to say much she did not press her.

"I can't press you to tell me the story, my child – my heart is full to the brim with story after story of you women who have suffered shame and cruelty in this city. You see those young women out there. They are secretaries and typists who want different jobs."

Elizabeth looked at Mrs Kimani with keen eyes. "That is what I want, help me find a different job even if it carries half my present salary."

"No, Liz, don't say that – you are one of our best secretaries, we can't lose you. Let us try Church Organisations this time Liz, don't give up too soon."

Elizabeth looked at Mrs Kimani with stray eyes – she liked her motherly advice, and she had helped many girls to get good jobs, but this time it was not her fault.

"Ma, remember how you talked to me when I left the American firm and the Wholesalers? You assured me that working for a fellow African with the country's progress at heart would be different. Ma, now that it has failed with the African, I have a strange feeling that it may not work even with Church Organisations. They all seem to be alike, inside the Church or outside. I have made up my mind."

"OK Liz, try these places. I will ring to tell them that you are calling this morning. Call on me if you are unsuccessful. And remember what I tell so many young people like you. Man has defied the laws of society; God alone will deal with him, and it has to be soon." Mrs Kimani watched Elizabeth disappear at the gate.

At the end of the week Elizabeth got a simple job with the Church Army, to care for destitute children in a small home. The work needed simplicity and patience. The woman in charge of the home asked her to shorten her nails. She had to wear a white overall, a white hair scarf and flat white shoes. One look at herself in the mirror nearly knocked her down.

"A nun? No, a nurse? No, no, no, a shop assistant? Oh no, an ayah? It looked like it. From a top grade secretary to an ayah!" Elizabeth tucked in a little flimsy hair that stuck out of the scarf near her ears. She followed Mother Hellena into a big hall where some thirty grubby-looking children were playing. Some were clay-modelling, some were painting while the smaller ones were playing with wooden bricks. Mother Hellena turned to Elizabeth.

"All these poor things have never known anything called love. They know they were brought into this world by somebody, but they don't know who! They hear other children like themselves have mothers and fathers, brothers and sisters, but they have nothing. What you and I can give them is what they will ever remember. Their whole future is in our hands."

All these eager and pathetic eyes were fixed upon Elizabeth and tears stung her eyes, for she knew she had no future to offer them. She herself had lost her bearings. She had escaped from the sophisticated life of the city hoping to find solace and comfort among the innocent children. Now they were all looking at her with yearning eyes, each one of them calling out to her, "Our future is in your hands, give us love and comfort which we have never known."

Elizabeth suppressed her tears and turned to Mother Hellena. "I did not know you had such a great task, Mother. I will offer them the little I have."

Ochola was shocked to hear about Elizabeth's new job. Her letter sounded pessimistic, but Ochola felt too guilty to press her. It was a mistake on his part to have allowed Elizabeth to return to Africa. He could have married her in the United States and they would have returned together as man and wife. But Elizabeth had insisted that she wanted to be married among her people and he gave in to her. Now with so many miles between them, Ochola found it difficult to be tough with her. He was returning home in five months time and he hoped to have everything under control.

Elizabeth struggled through the first week – the children were noisy, reckless and often rude. They had looked eager on her arrival, but now they resented her presence. She thought of ringing Mrs Kimani and telling her that she had changed her mind, but she could not bring herself to it. After one month the children started to like Elizabeth. Their pathetic gratitude made her at once humble and frustrated. The children needed so much more than she could give. She asked God to give her patience and understanding.

In the middle of June, Elizabeth felt very sick. Mother Hellena nursed her at home for two days but her position gradually deteriorated and she had to be admitted into hospital.

She spent three restless nights in hospital, but on the fourth day, Mother Hellena was allowed to talk to her. She was better and could eat. Mother Hellena pressed her hands tightly and looked away from her.

"Elizabeth, the doctor tells me that you are expecting a baby." The young woman's heart pounded painfully against her chest and she felt very hurt like a person suffering from a severe fever. The words played in her ears again. Did expecting a baby mean the same thing as being pregnant? She sat upright with a jerk and faced Mother Hellena.

"Did the doctor say so, did he say I am pr ... ?"

She let her lips close and ran a hand over her belly under the bed clothes. The confusion, the bitterness and the self reproach for what she regarded as personal failure had blotted everything out from Elizabeth's mind so that she had not realised she had missed two months. She grabbed Mother Hellena's arm and did not let go – she had to hold on to something. Violent pain was grabbing at her throat, her chest, her belly. The look on Mother Hellena's face could only be rebuke to her: "You are going to bring another unhappy, fatherless child into the world. Another destitute."

She recollected the admonition of the grandmother: "When a mature girl plays with boys and becomes pregnant outside of wedlock she brings much sadness to herself and to her family."

Exactly one month after leaving the hospital, Elizabeth made up her mind. Sooner or later Mother Hellena was going to get rid of her. The man she loved tenderly would not understand her even if she spoke with the tongue of angels. She could not return home to face her parents and grandmother. And she knew that firms did not like to employ pregnant women. The picture of Amy Jimbo came to her mind – it was the first time she had thought of her. Happy, contented and secure for life, when she, Elizabeth, in her tender age had no roof above her head. No, it was not fair. While Jimbo posed as an angel in the eyes of his wife, she, Elizabeth, was suffering shame and want – how heartless! She slipped her engagement ring on her finger and when the children were resting in the afternoon she dashed into town to have her hair done. As she sat lazily on the hair dresser's chair, the woman teased her.

"You have got a twinkle in your eyes. Are you meeting him tonight."

"Yes," Elizabeth whispered back.

"You are a beautiful woman, he is so lucky."

"Thank you – he is very handsome too, and kind."

The words resounded in her mind to mock her.

In the evening Elizabeth told Mother Hellena that she would spend the weekend with her uncle's family in town. She pulled out a notebook from her handbag and gave it to Mother Hellena. "Perhaps you may like to read about my childhood and my life in the city. I wrote it some time ago I will take it on Monday." She pressed Mother Hellena's hand and left to catch a bus to the city.

There was nobody at Mr Jimbo's home when Elizabeth got there – they might have taken the children for a drive, and perhaps the servants were spending their Sunday afternoon seeing friends. Elizabeth stood at the door for a while but the wind was biting around her ankles; it was going to rain. Presently she noticed the laundry room near the garage was open. She pulled a notebook from her handbag and scribbled a message: "I have come to stay, it is chilly standing at the door, so I thought I would wait for you in the laundry room. It is me, Elizabeth."

She tied the note on the door handle. The Jimbo family returned home just before sunset.

"Somebody has been visiting us," Amy said, opening the note. Then she read it aloud. Mr Jimbo snatched the note from his wife's hand. He tried to say something but only smothered meaningless sounds came out. Then he walked down to the laundry room in silence, while his wife, Amy, and the children stood dumbfounded near the door.

Jimbo flung the door open, and saw the body of a woman dangling on a red scarf. His feet gave way and he sagged to the ground.

"Quick, Amy, quick, the police please, an accident!" Dusk was gathering fast. The police were on their way to the house. They will probe, cross-examine and double-check their facts till they reach the truth, Jimbo thought. Oh my God, ending up like this!

Elizabeth Masaba's notebook was handed over to the police by Mother Hellena, and she knew she was doing the right thing. The Mother Superior thought grimly of all the other girls who were trapped in this way by those who are more powerful than they are.

Printed in the United States
By Bookmasters